also by
Jaap ter Haar

BORIS

# The World of Ben Lighthart

## by Jaap ter Haar

TRANSLATED FROM THE DUTCH BY MARTHA MEARNS

*A Merloyd Lawrence Book*

DELACORTE PRESS / SEYMOUR LAWRENCE

Originally published in Dutch under the title
HET WERELDJE VAN BEER LIGTHART
by Van Holkema and Warendorf, Bussum, Holland

Copyright © 1973 by Unieboek B.V., Bussum

English translation copyright © 1977 by
Dell Publishing Co., Inc.

Manufactured in the United States of America

First U.S. printing

Library of Congress Cataloging in Publication Data

Haar, Jaap ter, 1922–
      The world of Ben Lighthart.

      Translation of Het wereldje van Beer Ligthart
      "A Merloyd Lawrence book."
      SUMMARY: Blinded by accident, a young
boy decides he won't let his handicap keep him
from his friends and family.
      [1.  Blind—Fiction.  2.   Physically handicapped—
Fiction]    I.    Title.
PZ7.H1118Wo4      [Fic]        76-47236
ISBN 0-440-09684-7

# The World of Ben Lighthart

# Chapter One

A SPINE-CHILLING scream filled with fear and searing pain. Its echo resounded again and again and again.

"Ben!"

"Bennie!"

The voices of Peter and Jeff, close at hand, but as unearthly as whispers in an empty cathedral. Racing footsteps. The growl of traffic in the distance. And that pain, God, that pain. As he fell to the ground, Ben realized that it was he who had screamed. An incredible pain cut through him, and everything around him suddenly grew dim.

"A doctor! Get a doctor!"

Sounds seemed to be carried on the wind from another world, thin and unrecognizable. The wail of a siren. Something snapped. The blackness of a jungle. A universe full of color. And then nothing.

Ben found himself in a world of his own that kept expanding. His body didn't seem to be there, only that space in his skull full of hammering and bang-

I

ing and exploding fireworks, where trains collided and drums beat out the rhythm of a war dance. Then slowly this chaos of images and colors melted away. He heard the rustle of a stiff skirt and smelled the sharp, unmistakable smell of a hospital.

Was someone smoothing his hair?

It was dark. Ben tried to open his eyes, but it stayed dark and he felt a stabbing, blinding pain. His right hand, with its two bad bruises, moved back and forth restlessly over the sheet.

"Where am I?"

"We're here with you, Ben."

That was his father's voice and his father's trusted, comforting hand on his shoulder. Ben tried to struggle out of the confusing dream world in his head. He must open his eyes. Wake up. See Dad.

"My eyes! Where are my eyes?" Almost unconsciously he moved his hand from the sheet to his eye sockets. His fingers probed the thick bandage.

There was a sniff, a short sob, and then his mother's quiet voice.

"Darling, don't be afraid. I'm here, beside your bed."

"That pain . . . that pain." Ben didn't want to cry, to scream, but he couldn't stand it any longer. His fingers plucked more and more restlessly at the bandage.

"Nurse!" called his mother, her voice unsteady.

Nurse? Why a nurse?

The sheet was pulled back. Ben felt the sting of a shot in his thigh. His leg kicked out.

"Gently, darling, you needn't be afraid."

His mother's voice came from far, far away now. For a moment all Ben could feel was the glowing fever in his body, the thumping in his blood, and the pain, the devilish pain in his head. Suddenly he panicked. Was he going to die? He wanted to jump up, to hold on to something, to fight against death. A hand pushed him back, and the instant after death did not seem so terrible after all. He wasn't the first and he wouldn't be the last. All the same, there still remained an urge to fight for his life.

The unintelligible voices of his parents and the sounds of the sickroom drifted away out of reach. Ben sank back into a jungle of elusive figures, back into the universe full of color, into the thin emptiness, and then darkness.

No one knows the distance between life and death. So nobody knew how much of that road Ben had traveled, although the doctors and nurses realized that he was close to its end. Unconscious and in raging fever he was plunged into the fathomless world that lies hidden in the depths of every human being. There he wandered into black tunnels, saw threatening monsters, and felt strangled by a timeless fear. Then sometimes, there in the depths, he seemed to walk happily through pleasant green landscapes, for the innermost reaches of the soul of man are not entirely filled with misery. For two days and three nights Ben was unconscious nearly all the time. Sometimes he tossed and turned and raved. Sometimes a gentle, happy smile crept over the white face under its thick bandage. Then the nurse who

3

was on duty heard whispered words: "Please?" or "How beautiful!" And one time he said in a clear voice, "Thank you."

During the third night of that long journey from life to death his high fever began to sink. His breathing grew quieter and his heartbeat regained its former calm rhythm. Ben woke up on that third morning as if he had been awakened from a dreaming, bottomless sleep. It was only gradually that he realized he was really awake. His mouth was parched and he felt a great thirst. The pain came back, but it was not so devilish as before.

*Pain . . . ?* Slowly, shadowy memories returned: the quiet voice of his mother, his father's hand, and the vague images that had flitted across the screen of his dream.

Footsteps came closer. They rang sharp and hollow on the hard floor. Someone drew open the curtains. You could hear that from the metallic rattle. *Something isn't right*, thought Ben. The room was still shrouded in darkness.

"Is that you, Mom?"

His mother could surely explain those strange noises, the pain, and that sickly, nauseating smell.

"Where am I?"

A cool hand clasped his arm.

"You're in the hospital, Ben. I'm your nurse, nurse Win."

Hospital? Nurse Win? Ben didn't understand.

He tried desperately to find some support. Yes, school was over. Peter had been grumbling about the French test, and Jeff had been fooling around

4

with a ball and then he had made that crooked pass. And then . . . ? Hadn't he, Ben, dashed into the street after the ball? And stumbled over Jeff's bag? The picture wouldn't come clearer.

"What happened?"

"You had an accident after school."

"An accident?"

Had he been knocked down? Then he must be pretty shattered. Hesitatingly Ben moved his legs, then his arms. Thank God, they didn't hurt. They were still whole.

"Your parents will be coming soon. They know what happened. I wasn't there, you know."

Ben felt the bandage round his head again. Of course! That was it, that was why he couldn't see anything. He felt his shoulders, his thighs, his chest. Everything seemed in good order.

"Would you like something to drink?"

"Thanks, nurse."

The nurse's voice sounded clear, friendly, and firm. She knew what she was doing. Ben tried to sit up, but at once the pain thumped in his eyes and through the whole of his head.

"Just lie still, I'll use a cup with a spout."

Something like the spout of a teapot was inserted in his mouth. Weak tea. He took a few sips. That really helped his parched mouth.

"Thanks a lot," he said from the bottom of his heart as he tried to put his thoughts in order.

"I have to go away for a moment," said the nurse's voice. "Try to get some sleep."

Rustle of a skirt. Clink of a cup and saucer. Foot-

5

steps going to the door. Ben was alone again, surrounded by vague hospital sounds. Which hospital? And how long would he have to stay there?

"Stupid, I should have asked," he muttered to himself.

He also wanted to know when they would free him from that thick, suffocating bandage because he didn't like that endless darkness at all. And he'd very much like to see that nurse Win. She'd be sure to have blond hair and blue eyes and a plentiful bosom under her white uniform. You could hear it in her voice.

Ben lay very still now. He was trying to recall what had happened to him after school.

Jeff had given the ball a shove . . . yes, the accident must have happened right after. Had a car got him? *If so, I've been lucky*, thought Ben, for his body was still all in one piece. Had he gone head-first through a car window? Was that why his head was bandaged? Suddenly a shocking thought flashed through him, putting an end to all the doubt and uncertainty.

There are things that children sometimes know in a flash. Thoughts well up from nowhere, and they feel absolutely sure they are right. Although there is not a shred of evidence, still they sense the truth— with a kind of second sight lost to most adults.

Such a moment of certainty, such an instant of truth, came to Ben Lighthart. All at once he remembered that he had called out in the midst of pain and dreams. Again he heard his own fearful voice:

"My eyes? Where are my eyes?"

And suddenly he realized with heartrending clarity that he would never see his blond nurse Win in reality. That he would never again see his parents, his sister Maryanne, his school, and his friends. Never again would he enjoy a baseball match, television, or the soft green richness of a wood in spring. The sun would never rise for him again. There was no longer any doubt about it at all, only certainty.

"Oh, God, I'm blind," came Ben's shocked whisper, and he didn't know how he was to live with himself.

It was quite a while before the nurse came back. Ben had time to think about the truth he had just established for himself. It was not easy.

In that dark world under the bandage all sorts of thoughts and images fluttered around.

Blind! He remembered the man with the dark glasses and a white stick whom he'd seen shuffling helplessly along a busy shopping street. From now on he'd have to find his way like that, at home, at school, wherever he was. For the rest of his life he'd be dependent on other people.

Ben closed his fists defiantly and then thought, *But wasn't everybody somehow dependent on other people?*

Blind! Suddenly he was seized by terror. Would they send him to some institute for the blind? No, that mustn't happen. It couldn't happen. Ben thought about his father and mother and their ever more serious rows, in which he sometimes stood between them. Wasn't there a big chance that they'd part for good if he wasn't there any more? That thought was unbearable. Then it suddenly shot through him— how terrible it would be for his parents that he was blind. Did they already know?

Blind! Darn it, he wouldn't cry. He could take it. He remembered something he'd once said long ago to his mother: "If you're the most pathetic kid in the world you don't have to be sorry for anyone else." That was when he'd been so upset about children hurt and crippled by war. Or about children not old enough to walk maimed by leprosy. Or perhaps it had been when he'd seen television shots of the bewildered victims of a famine.

Blind! It was terrible, but there were still more terrible things in the world. He still had a future. He'd have to learn braille. He'd have to mold his life in a completely new pattern. At the same time as he thought about it all, Ben was amazed that he could accept his blindness reasonably calmly.

Footsteps in the corridor. The soft click of the opening door. The voice of nurse Win.

"Here I am again, Ben."

Something was put on the table (or was it a cabinet) next to his bed.

"Nurse?"

"Yes?"

"I'm blind, aren't I? For always."

Silence for a moment. Ben heard the nurse breathing. He hoped with all his heart she'd give him an honest answer. The truth was easier to bear than uncertainty and false hopes.

Luckily, nurse Win was wise enough to know that

most children are pretty brave and can accept all kinds of circumstances as long as they're not thrown into confusion by adults.

"Yes," she said, and Ben again felt her cool hand on his arm. "Both your eyes are so badly damaged that you will probably never be able to see again."

"Thank you," said Ben. He was truly grateful she hadn't thought up an excuse and left him with the uncertainty of a half answer. Wasn't it odd that he found nurse Win swell and he'd never even seen her?

"Here's your breakfast. An egg and toast and honey. Shall we try, the two of us, to get something inside?"

"Yes," replied Ben. It was good to know that life— even if you were blind—went on as usual. Soon his mother and father would come. He'd tell them the truth at once. Quite matter-of-fact, just like nurse Win. Perhaps then they wouldn't be so shocked.

The door opened with a sound like a puff of wind. Ben was already getting used to it.

The voice of nurse Win, still clear, still friendly, still very matter-of-fact.

"Ben, your parents are here."

Now it was Ben's turn to take a deep breath. He put his hand out to the right, but it turned out that Mother was already at the other side of the bed. From the left came a kiss on his cheek and her voice, hoarse and nervous:

"Oh, darling. Ben dear . . . "

It was his father who took his hand. So there was one on either side of the bed.

"Well, Ben. Here we are again. Good that you've come round. Last time we were here you were out for the count."

"Yes," nodded Ben, wondering how to begin to tell them.

"How are you feeling now, darling?"

He could hear that his mother was trying hard to make her voice sound as natural as possible. It was as unnatural as a green moon.

"The pain's not so bad."

"Is the nurse nice?"

"Yes," said Ben, and then he put a stop to all this pointless circling around the unavoidable truth.

"You know that I'm blind, don't you? For good?"

There was an audible swallow. He felt his mother's hand grasp his wrist as if to find strength.

"Yes, Ben, we know," said his father. "Only we didn't know that you knew too. We intended to tell you when you were a bit stronger."

"Darling," began Mother, and then she stopped. His father finished the sentence for her.

"We've been given a load to carry among us, and there's nothing else to do but carry it."

"Among us?"

"Yes, of course. Your mother and you and I."

Ben felt tears coming then and he was glad that there was a bandage over his eyes. He bit his lip and said softly:

"Funny, this morning I wasn't afraid of being blind, but of you two . . . "

"Go on."

"Of you two leaving each other."

The words were heavy as lead. They seemed to hang over the bed like a thundercloud of reproach.

"Dear God," whispered his mother. "Our own son."

Ben knew for sure that she was looking at his father.

Now Mother couldn't burst into tears and Dad couldn't think up some smooth excuse to evade this important issue. It was his father who sat on the edge of the bed and broke the silence:

"Ben, every marriage hangs at times on a silken thread. Like ours, your mother's and mine, as you've already understood. But thank God, most silken threads are rather strong."

It was an honest answer, giving sufficient hope for the future, and there seemed nothing more to be said.

"Will you tell me now what happened to me?" asked Ben. There were still so many blank spaces in his thoughts that needed filling.

Now it was his mother who answered, in her usual, quiet voice. And so Ben heard how on the way home from school he'd jumped into the street after a ball without looking, he'd stumbled, he'd fallen with his head on the sharp rake carried by a gardener who was passing on a motorbike and had no time to swerve.

"The gardener couldn't do a thing," added his father.

"He's been along twice to ask about you. He feels terrible."

Ben lying unconscious after the accident. The

ambulance ride to the hospital. Then on a stretcher to the clinic. His parents' long, terrible wait for the doctor's verdict.

"Then you came to, just for a moment."

"Yes, I know that."

Ben vaguely remembered that instant, filled with the terror of dying. Right afterward he'd sunk back into unconsciousness.

His mother told him briefly about the operation and the fever that had followed. In a few minutes the missing two days and three nights were bridged with words.

Luckily, nurse Win came in then to say that the visit had gone on long enough. Ben felt dead tired and the thumping and the pain in his head were nearly unbearable. When his parents had gone, tears burst out. The tensions and emotions that he'd had to undergo in such a short time were just too much.

"Yes, go on and cry," said the voice of nurse Win. "You always feel better afterward." She didn't try to comfort him, but let him be. Because of that the fit of crying was soon over, but the stabbing, burning pain under the bandage wasn't any less.

"Ben, I'm going to give you an injection for the pain. You'll be off again in no time."

A few moments later the sounds disappeared, and the sickroom, the bed, and the pain seemed to dissolve. Ben drifted with painless, pleasant dreaming thoughts toward the unknown future.

# Chapter Two

LIFE in the hospital had a rhythm of its own. When the pain grew less Ben discovered that the hours of the day could be expressed in sounds.

You could hear the start of a new day when the curtains were pulled open and the thermometers were given out. It didn't matter to Ben whether his curtains were open or shut, so they stayed open.

Sounds from the kitchen of plates, cups, knives, and forks being laid on trays announced that breakfast was being prepared. From the rattle of a trolley with instruments Ben knew that a doctor was making his rounds and so it must be ten o'clock. A stream of footsteps in the corridor and the rustle of the paper wrapped round bunches of flowers made it clear that visiting hours had begun. That was when his mother came, two or three minutes after two. At night there were specific sounds in the silence: the swish of a nurse's skirt as she walked round seeing that everything was in order or the buzz of a push button when a patient asked for something. Sometimes running feet and urgent whispering of

13

nurses and doctors in the corridor made Ben know that one of the patients must be in a bad way. All those sounds pushed their way into his dark world like small messengers, with the result that he began more and more to see with his ears.

Every time nurse Win came in it was as if a light filled his sickroom. She was quite a person, and he couldn't have gotten through the long hours without her. Difficult times came when nurse Win had her day off and another nurse took her place.

*Nurse Annie must look like a duck*, thought Ben. Her constantly cheerful voice gave him the creeps. Quack, quack, quack. She didn't ring true, and everything she said seemed to evade reality. It was irritating.

"Now we're going to have a lovely wash," she'd sing out, as if all that sploshing around with soap and water was great fun.

"And now it's time for the potty." With an ungentle jerk his pajama pants were round his knees, and bang, an ice-cold bedpan was shoved under his bottom.

"And now for something nice to eat." She didn't mention what was on the plate but immediately pushed a lump of broccoli into his mouth. It was one thing Ben couldn't stand, broccoli. With the courage of despair he swallowed down the first mouthful, while nurse Annie, quack, quack, quack, chattered and giggled, though there didn't seem much to laugh about.

On those days Ben sank deeper into the slough. He felt more lonely and desperate than he had ever been, and all the circumstances of his future life seemed more and more black.

Blind! Why had this had to happen to him? He already saw himself staggering around in the future: helped along by his father or mother, hashing his meals around, dependent on everyone.

Blind! Only pity and charity would be his lot from now on. How would he ever get himself a girl? What woman would ever get involved with a blind, stumbling bungler?

When his father came to visit him that evening, Ben's courage and good humor had sunk to below zero. He tried not to let it show, because his father, he thought, had it hard enough already. And so he restrained himself and tried to talk casually of this and that. But when nurse Annie came in with his hot drink and had a chat with his father in that oh-so-sweet, cheerful voice, then it was too much.

"What a sweetie," said his father when she'd disappeared along the corridor.

"She's a nitwit!" Ben spat out the words venomously.

"Say that again!" His father's voice was genuinely surprised. "She looks a bit of all right to me," he said, then clamped his mouth shut, as if he wanted to bite off his tongue.

"All the same, she's a nitwit. I couldn't care less how she looks." All his hopelessness came pouring out with the words.

"I get it," mumbled his father, rather shakily.

A short, painful silence followed. Then his father's voice said quietly, almost carefully:

15

"You know, Ben, our eyes often distract us from the important things. With them we notice all sorts of details that have nothing to do with the matter in hand. We go by people's outward appearance, which really isn't at all important. That mistake won't be yours from now on. Can you understand that it can be an advantage? Far more than other people you'll be able to sense how people really are. Maybe you're right and that pretty nurse is a nitwit after all."

However good his father's intention, Ben was not in the mood to find solace in that sort of fine, uplifting preaching. Inside he stayed mulish and so felt still more hopeless and disheartened.

His father understood. He did his best to fill the rest of the hour with stories about his work and described all of a television program he'd seen the evening before. Only when he said good-bye did he try once again to give his son the moral support he seemed to need so badly:

"Ben, of one thing I'm sure. You'll get through. I'm not going to pretend that it will be easy, but believe me, we'll make it."

Ben felt a kiss just under his bandage and the faint roughness of his father's skin.

"You're a tough guy. The worst is over."

No, Ben half whispered to himself after his father had gone, the worst had just begun. Only now did he begin to realize the futility of being blind.

A few minutes later, nurse Annie came in to get him ready for the night.

"Now we're going to tuck you up all cozy and warm."

Quack, quack, quack! Of course the stupid duck drew the curtains.

"Sleep tight, laddie."

Laddie! He could almost hear the "poor" before it. With clenched fists Ben punched his pillow, and, sniffing with self-pity, he muttered inaudibly:

"Oh, God, if you exist, help me . . . "

A restless night. Like runaway horses, terrifying dreams raced through his sleep.

The deathly stillness of a frozen lake. Gathering dusk. Skating along past gaps and continually breaking ice. Crack. Still more crevices filling with water under his feet. And he couldn't see the thin patches.

To the left. Quick, to the right. At last, in spite of all his efforts, the wrong turning . . . the ice broke and he sank into the dark depths. . . .

Ben awoke in a cold sweat. Gradually the oppressive fear slid away from him. The darkness filled with the vague sounds of the hospital: the smothered giggles of two night nurses in the kitchen, a buzzer, footsteps, more footsteps and whispering voices. A few minutes later a trolley with a stretcher passed by, its wheels softly squeaking. An emergency operation?

Ben dropped off to sleep again—and again a dream was inescapably with him.

He was at home alone with Maryanne. He was looking through a window at hundreds of black snakes slithering over the lawn and through the flowers. Were they trying to get into the house? Were they searching for Maryanne?

Help, a window was open. Panic-stricken, he raced to the living room to shut it. Too late! A thick snake was already halfway over the sill and was thrusting its horrid head menacingly forward. He raced back to shut the door to the hall. Maryanne pointed to the kitchen. There was a window open there, too, and he raced toward it. Again, too late! Twisting and turning over each other, the snakes wriggled inside. Back! He pulled Maryanne upstairs after him. It must still be safe up there. He stormed into the bathroom, but already the bath was filled with black snakes. Maryanne was horrified and pressed her hands over her eyes . . .

Again Ben woke with a start. He sat up to have a look round. He wanted to know for sure it was only a dream. It was only when he was sitting bolt upright in bed that it struck him that he could see nothing. It stayed pitch dark all around him . . .

Blind! He sank back on his pillow and thought about everything that was lost beyond recall for him. No more sports. No more jumping on his bike to drop in on a friend. No chance now of becoming a doctor as he'd always wanted. Even more dejected than he had been up till now, he waited for the sounds of the new day.

Footsteps. The breeze caused by the opening door. Was it nurse Win who was now quietly drawing the curtains?

"Nurse Win?" He heard the fear and despair in his voice.

"Good morning, Ben. Is there anything wrong?"

As she walked toward him, Ben pulled himself up and cried frantically:

"Nurse Win, my life, my whole life's ruined!"

"But, Ben . . . " Nurse Win put an arm round his shoulders. Her voice was as calm as ever, as if a ruined life was the most everyday thing in the world.

"But, Ben, everybody says that at one time or another. Me too—I've said something like that more than once. But of course it's never true. There's always a new beginning right ahead."

"Yes, it's easy for you to talk. You've still got your eyes. You can still see."

There was a moment's silence. Tense silence. Then nurse Win took Ben's hand and slowly raised it.

"Feel my cheek carefully with your fingers—yes, right there. Do you feel those leathery wrinkles from my eyes to my chin?"

"Yes," whispered Ben in a shaken voice.

"The right half of my face was burned when I was fifteen. I had just fallen in love with someone who never gave me another glance. I look very unattractive, you know. Most patients give a start when they see me for the first time."

"Oh, nurse . . . "

Stammered words because Ben didn't know what to say.

"Don't worry about it, Ben. My brown leather

cheek is no great tragedy. It's a small tragedy, like millions of others in the world. Take care that your blindness stays a small tragedy, Ben, for otherwise you'll have no life at all."

Nurse Win fixed his pillows for him and took longer than usual to tidy his sickroom. She was giving Ben plenty of time to sweep together the shreds of the past twenty-four hours.

A new beginning. Now Ben felt ashamed that he had lost control, for he wasn't the most pitiful being in the world. Far from it. Wasn't it now about time to say good-bye to the rebellious, embittered, complaining boy he'd shown himself to be in the last hours?

Pulling himself together—for everyone has to struggle through his own tragedies—he silently decided to take his place on the starting line of a new kind of life.

"Ben," said nurse Win, and he had quite forgotten that she was in the room, "whatever happens, there is always something to be thankful for. Really and truly. With a bit of thankfulness you have a much more pleasant existence than with miserable discontent. And now I'm going to fetch your breakfast."

Ben saw her go in his imagination: fair, blue-eyed, and infinitely more beautiful than pretty nurse Annie in spite of that brown, burned, leathery cheek.

Now in the dark world under the thick bandage all sorts of things began to shift around. The more Ben thought over everything, the better he saw that not everything was lost. Another life was waiting for him, that was for sure. A life of feeling with his fingers, of listening to voices and sounds. From now on his hands and his ears and his nose would have to do the work of his eyes.

Being blind was turning out to be different than he had imagined. He had always thought that blindness would cut a person's life in half and that he would be doomed to helplessness. Now he realized that he was almost the same Ben as before.

Maryanne, who was only nine, couldn't understand that. For her, blindness was a total catastrophe.

"Oh, Ben, I think it's so awful for you," she had almost sobbed when she first came to see him in hospital.

"It isn't so terrible as all that," he had answered. "Being blind is like sitting in a cinema. You're in the dark, but you see everything happening on the screen. That's what it's like for me. There are lots of pictures passing by under this bandage."

That was the truth. In his thoughts he saw the sickroom around him. With nurse Win. She was very clear. And the doctor, too, who came on his rounds each morning and surely had gray hair and glasses. How lucky, thought Ben, that he hadn't been born blind, for then all the images under the bandage would have been far less sharp.

One afternoon the gardener had come to visit him, bringing a bowl of hyacinths.

"A bit of spring for you to sniff at. Maybe it will get rid of some of the hospital smell."

Although he'd never met him, Ben could see the gardener quite clearly before him: a gentle man with strong, callused hands, with fingers that couldn't pick up postage stamps because they'd become hardened by his work. They talked over the accident:

"It's a devil of a business."

"You couldn't help it," said Ben quickly. "I've asked myself ten times over why I jumped into the street without looking."

"Never ask why, Ben. Your whole life long you'll get no answer. In the garden where I work there are two mighty oaks. I call them the Siamese twins because the lowest branch of the one tree—as thick as my thigh—is also the lowest branch of the other one. Why? Things happen, Ben. You learn that in a garden. And by working hard among them you prevent that garden from becoming one big tangle."

Ben too had seen clearly the two united oaks. And later, when he lay alone after that visiting hour, just like a movie he saw the gardener working near the oaks: weeding, pruning, pushing along the wheelbarrow with his steady gardener's gait, busy among the bushes and shrubs he'd planted round a pond.

Fantasy? For Ben it was an experience. If you were blind the world didn't have to grow smaller. In your thoughts you could make it just as big, beautiful, or ugly as you wanted.

After a week, when the pains had more or less disappeared, Ben had to move to a ward. He got a shock when he heard that. He felt far from ready to have strangers before his blind eyes. And what was worse, he wouldn't see nurse Win any more. See . . . ? Well, have her around.

"I'll come and see you, of course," promised nurse Win, when she had hoisted him onto the stretcher for removal to ward three. She pushed him out of the room. The wheels squeaked as usual. Along the hall and into an elevator going down. Again along a hall and around a corner. Then they stopped. A door opened and his ears met the buzz of men's voices punctuated by bursts of laughter. The sounds broke off as he was wheeled through the door.

"God in heaven." In the sudden silence Ben's sense of blindness again gripped him by the throat. Afraid and insecure, now he was rolled on the stretcher through ward three to his new bed.

How many men lay in the ward? Were they all now looking at him?

"Jesus, Mary, and Joseph," came a whisper from a corner, and the silence seemed to deepen.

"Ben, I'm going to pull you over. Put your arm round my neck."

The clear voice of nurse Win cut into the emptiness. He was pulled up and gently pushed back onto the pillows. Then he heard his belongings being put on the cabinet by the bed. The bowl of hyacinths, the basket of fruit from his class.

"Oh, how stupid. I've forgotten your radio." Ben had been given a transistor radio with headphones by his parents. He could listen to plays and music without disturbing the others.

"I'll get it right away," said nurse Win, and she was gone. Ben felt even more afraid and alone.

Where was he now? Who was lying around him? Then a voice reached him from close by, rough but friendly:

"Hi, kid, I'm your neighbor, Jerry. I'm stuck here with two smashed feet because an anchor chain got me. Next to me is Grandad Abe, a parasite who does nothing but yatter on about his appendix. So I'm glad to have you on my other side."

Ben didn't see a hand unthinkingly stretched out in greeting and that hand quickly withdrawn.

"Hey, shall I tell you who else there is? Now that you're here, there are six of us."

"Please do," mumbled Ben, still rather embarrassed. He didn't know how to act in the new situation.

"In the corner by the window—that's to your right—is the baker. He's had a stomach operation and won't laugh, for he nearly bursts with the pain. You should see how scared he looks if we start telling jokes. His wife just about kills us with cookies and cakes, so all in all we're pretty glad to have him around."

Ben saw the baker before him. No doubt like most bakers he had a dough-white face.

"Across in the middle is his lordship, sitting up in bed wearing pure silk pajamas in bright orange that he loves to show off to all comers."

"For heaven's sake, Jerry," a super-well-bred voice exploded, "I've told you at least five times that my dearest wife bought the ghastly garments."

"He looks like a goldfish very much out of its element."

24

Ben laughed. He couldn't see the glance of triumph Jerry gave the others as he nodded to the broad grin under the bandage.

"The rustling of papers across from you comes from a student in sickology." Ben grinned again. "He's sick enough—something wrong with his kidneys, to judge from the number of times he needs a bottle. The last bed's still empty. But if another old blatherer like Grandad Abe gets it, I'm walking out, broken bones and all!"

When nurse Win came back with the radio, Ben already felt a little bit at home in ward three, thanks to the sailor who, with a few rough and ready sentences, had brought a measure of calm to that small, insecure world under the bandage. It was as if he'd gotten over the first obstacle on the long road full of obstacles that stretched before him.

# Chapter
# Three

W*HERE am I?* thought Ben when he awoke the next morning. He was aware, still half asleep as he was, that he was no longer in his small room. Oh, yes, he remembered. He'd been moved to ward three.

It was quiet. Were the others still asleep? He heard Jerry's heavy breathing next to him. A restless, gurgling kind of sound came from the baker in the corner.

Was it already morning? Or still the middle of the night? Only the radio could give him the answer. Ben sat up. Tentatively he put his hand out to the cabinet. As he did so his wrist met something cold. Clatter and whoosh. Then a crash of glass and the trickling of water.

"Hey . . . ho." Jerry shot up in bed, forgetting that his damaged feet were heavily bandaged. There was a splutter of oaths. "Hell's bells!"

Beds creaked. Covers rustled. Ward three had been rudely awakened.

"What happened?"

"Did something fall?"

"What was that crash?"

Ben was painfully aware that in his blindness he'd committed a clumsy blunder.

"I bumped against something. Here the cabinet's more to the front of the bed than my last one," he stammered apologetically.

"You tumbled a vase of daffodils," explained Jerry. "I got the flowers and a load of water over me. Nurse'll think I've wet my bed."

"Gee, I'm sorry."

"Don't be daft, Ben. There's nothing to be sorry about. I've never been woken with flowers before!"

"Is it morning yet? Or is it still night?"

"Ten past six precisely," said his lordship in his precise voice. "The nurses will be coming any minute with their thermometers, washbasins, and gentle morning mood."

And they came, nurse Ruth and nurse Rose. From the sounds Ben deduced that his lordship and Grandad Abe—for whom it was the last day—went to the washroom to wash. The rest got their daily scrubbing from the nurses. It didn't seem to suit Jerry too well.

"Aw, nurse, not so hard. How about the touch of a gentle hand? And you don't have to turn up your nose like that—I haven't got cobwebs in my behind, have I?"

"No, Jerry," nurse Ruth had an answer in a flash. "Your tongue's a lot dirtier than your bottom."

"Well said, nurse," called his lordship. "She wins, Jerry, one to the ladies."

"Women," groaned Jerry to Ben.

Time in ward three slipped past much faster than in the small sickroom. It was a strange word to use, *slip*. Yet it did describe what happened to days in the hospital. They really did slip past because ward three was like a waiting room, a pause between past and future. Real life seemed to stand still.

Not that they didn't have fun. From dawn to dusk jests and jokes were thrown about the room. Especially when the baker had to laugh—and at the same time groan with pain—everyone else had to hold their sides too.

"Stop it now, ho, ho, ho, ooh, ow, hoo, hoo, hoo . . . ow, ow . . . stop it . . . "

The baker almost choked trying to control his uncontrollable giggles. Ben could see him plainly, supporting his painfully heaving stomach with both hands.

Once in a while the voice of the student would break in: "Couldn't you people be quiet just for a minute?"

*He must want to study*, thought Ben, and of course he couldn't in all that row.

"Throw those books away" was the advice of Jerry, who honestly admitted he'd never read a book in his life.

There were also moments when the fun and foolery were suddenly stilled to deep earnestness. Then it was usually the student who spoke about life with calmness and wisdom. And then Ben would think that psychology must be a really fine subject: unraveling the knots and tangled threads of some confused skein of human life. Could someone who was blind become a psychologist? Did textbooks in braille exist?

New questions kept occurring to Ben and with them new uncertainties and fears.

The second morning in ward three Ben was allowed up for the first time. His feet slipping from under him—what was a queer feeling—he stood unsteadily on the floor. It was only by leaning heavily on nurse Ruth's plump arm that he managed to complete his first walk round his bed. In the afternoon he had to try it alone. Jerry shouted encouragement.

"Come on, Bennie. Straight ahead, kid. There's nothing in the way."

To please Jerry, Ben stepped forward a little too bravely, past the foot of the bed. He lost contact with it. He stood still, feeling into emptiness with his hands and with the panicky feeling that any minute he would stumble over something. Lost and afraid, he stood there, and the darkness under the bandage paralyzed him more than ever. He felt dizzy. It seemed as if the floor began to tilt, and with his next step he lost his balance.

"Don't panic," said the voice of the student, who caught him and held him up. "If you're not nervous, you'll be much steadier on your feet."

"I'm so dizzy."

"I'll take you back to your bed. This way . . . that's it . . . " The student's arm slid round him protectingly. A moment later Ben felt the safety of his bed under him again. He was nearer to tears than laughter, for he'd never felt so desperately helpless.

"What a lot we are," barked Jerry, unable to swallow his feelings. "The baker can't laugh, his lordship can't eat, I can't walk, and Ben can't see. The only one that can do everything is the student."

"Surely you're not jealous, Jerry."

"Am I ever!"

"You shouldn't be," said the student, and his voice sounded sad. Two days later Ben was to discover why.

The rain spattered against the windows, and a strong wind howled round the walls of the hospital. It was one of those rare moments of quiet in ward three. Jerry was asleep. Perhaps he'd had a bad night and was making up for it now. The baker was leafing through a magazine. There was a rustle as he turned each page. His lordship's pen scratched over a writing pad—with a sharp tick when he put a period at the end of a sentence.

*A small world of noises*, thought Ben. His imagination had to do the rest. Was that enough?

"Keep fighting for your independence, Ben," the student had said one afternoon. How were you supposed to do that, if you couldn't see a glimmer of light? Could he find on his own, for instance, the way from his home to his school? In his thoughts Ben walked out of his house. The brick path to the gate. Then to the right. Yes, if you felt along the edge of the sidewalk with a stick you couldn't go wrong.

Except by Beech Avenue there were trees along the street. Could you avoid collisions by swinging the stick out ahead of you?

On the way home from school he'd have to cross a street four, no, five times. Could he do that on his own? *Of course, you'd first have to listen to the traffic,* thought Ben. *When you didn't hear any more cars and motorbikes, then you'd have to shove out the white stick and, "Look out, everybody, here I come."*

People would look at him all right and find him pathetic, for to begin with, that crossing of the street would proceed very awkwardly.

"You'll have to harden yourself against people's pity," the student had said yesterday with emphasis. "Keep on letting everyone see that you're not pathetic. Don't let your life be wrecked by the people around you."

Of course, the student was right. With a bit of resourcefulness you could get around a number of obstacles. Ben fully realized that he wouldn't be able to do a great number of things. Cycling, for instance. Would he from now on always have to get a lift from someone else? Someone tapped him on the arm. Ben jumped because it was so unexpected.

"I've come for a chat."

It was the student. He spoke softly so as not to disturb the others.

"Don't you want to study? It's nice and quiet now."

"I'm not in the mood for my books."

"Is it difficult?"

"It's not that, it's . . . " His reply remained hanging in midsentence.

"Do you still have long to study?"

"No," and again the student's voice sounded sad. "In a few weeks I'll be finished with everything."

*There's something not right*, thought Ben. How he'd have liked to see the student's face, just for a moment. There was something in his voice that gave the words a deeper meaning. Was Ben being told something that he didn't understand?

"Aren't you glad that you're so near the end of your studies?"

"It's not only that, Ben. I'm near the end of everything."

For a brief moment these words slipped past Ben. Then the devastating truth slowly penetrated.

"You mean . . . no, you can't mean . . . " Shocked and bewildered, Ben caught his breath.

The student gripped his arm. When he spoke again it was with his usual quiet intimacy to which Ben had grown accustomed.

"Yes, that's what I mean. My end is near at hand. I've only a few more weeks ahead of me."

"But . . . "

"You mustn't be shocked, Ben. I'm not the first and I won't be the last. We always think of death as a frightful enemy. But if you're very close to it, like me, it turns out to be a loving friend."

"I . . . " Ben didn't know what to say. A lump came into his throat.

"Don't tell the others. Let it stay a secret between you and me."

"But . . . " Ben swallowed the lump. "Why are you telling me this?"

"Because it can help you. Because if death can be a loving friend, blindness can certainly grow to be a good companion. I would so much like you to keep on loving life, Ben, even if it sometimes lets you down."

"Hey!" Jerry had woken up and turned over in bed. "What are you two cooking up between you?"

"Oh, nothing special." The student said the words so quietly, as if dying weren't something very special indeed. Now he was surely looking toward the next bed with a smile.

"Bah," mumbled Jerry. "To think I have to see your glum puss now of all times. I was dreaming of a gorgeous girl. Blond, with everything in the right place. She said, 'Gerald, come closer to me.' And I walked right up to her, just as if my feet weren't kaput."

"If I were you, I'd go right back to sleep. Maybe your honey of a girl will come back to you." The student laughed, while Ben felt like crying.

"Oh, man, drop dead," Jerry growled, half to himself.

The slang cut Ben to the heart. For a few seconds it was as if heaven wept too, for the wind howled and another squall of rain burst in spatters against the windows.

"At least we're lying high and dry," said the baker. It was scant comfort.

That evening sleep wouldn't come. Again and

again Ben thought of what the student had said to him.

To die. That seemed the worst of all. But why? Life was so essentially fine, wasn't it? And again, why?

Ben tried to make a list of the best things in his life.

Vacation, but some were better than others.

Having a birthday. Well, so so.

Sports. Yet lots of people took no interest.

Halloween. Christmas. New Year. All fine and jolly, but certainly not vital days.

"No," muttered Ben. Such a list wasn't the answer. Those weren't the things for which you especially wanted to live. On the other hand, you could easily make a list of rotten things; they came to mind much more quickly.

War, such as in Vietnam.

Dying—and the student was still so young.

Father and mother getting divorced.

John across the road, who was spastic and always sat in a wheelchair.

Poverty, hunger. And knowing that three-quarters of the earth's population had to undergo poverty and hunger.

"Strange," whispered Ben aloud. There were more nasty, sad, and horrible things in the world than fine. But you didn't want to die because of that.

Then what made life so worth living? That you loved your father and mother, even if at times they didn't love each other? And Maryanne? And Jeff and Pete . . . ?

Yes, that was it. What you couldn't do without in life was the people you loved. All the other things— the finest and the most rotten—took second place.

"Wow," said Ben, with a sense of relief. Even though he was blind now, the essential thing wasn't lost. Because you could still love people even if you couldn't see them.

The days slipped by: the morning sounds, thermometers and washbasins. The slop of a wet mop on the floor. The doctor's rounds. The thick bandage, sticky and tickly, was changed, thank goodness, for a smaller one, fixed at the sides of his eyes with tape. The afternoon sounds: lunch being brought, then the clatter of knives and forks on plates. And the complaining voice of his lordship:

"I simply can't eat it."

Ben was usually fed by nurse Ruth and sometimes by the student, who was allowed out of bed to do so.

"Try to eat by yourself now," he said one day. "The meat's on the right side of your plate cut in pieces. I've mashed up the rest."

"But I'll make a mess." Ben tried to get out of it.

"What does that matter? Later you'll eat without messing."

"I can't see it."

"You can still feel, can't you? Bats are blind, too, yet they still manage to fly safely among trees, between the branches, or along a wall or over a roof. Do you know why?"

"No, why?"

"Each object sends out signals and they receive

them perfectly. I think a person's got a similar radar system. Take care to develop it, Ben. With it you'll win your independence."

"Do you think I can do it?"

"Of course. I've seen people who were almost blind playing basketball. Just imagine that—two teams in a big hall. Players that can hardly see. Yet they find the ball. They score. People can hardly understand how it's done. Yet it happens. They hear the ball bouncing. They sense where their opponents are."

Ben had picked up his fork. Pushing, probing, and pricking—and without so much mess after all—he managed to get his first independent warm meal inside him.

Afterward the student led him to the corridor. Suddenly he let go of Ben's arm.

"Going to walk by yourself?"

"But . . ."

"Come on, you can do it. Forward, right ahead."

Ben cautiously shuffled forward, but all at once he stopped.

"Why don't you go on?"

"I . . . I've got the feeling there's something there." Ben stretched out a hand and, sure enough, before him was a wall.

"You see?" cried the student triumphantly. "You see, you sensed it!"

Ben was not yet fully convinced, but it was a fact that he'd stopped just before that wall.

The afternoon sounds: first the afternoon nap with Jerry's heavy snoring. Then the shuffle of feet in the corridor. Voices and the rustling of paper wrappings around flowers and candies announced that visiting hour had begun. Mother came then, sometimes with Grandma and sometimes with Maryanne.

"Who's that funny-looking man with the long hair and the beard?" Grandma whispered one day.

"He's not one of us," answered Ben.

"Of course he is, dear. Across from you, in the left corner."

It was only then that Ben realized that Grandma meant the student. He got a shock, because he'd imagined the student to be quite different. And again the hard truth struck him, that people judge other people so rashly on their outward appearance: on a beard and long hair, on a neat business suit, on a short skirt or a see-through blouse. Because of a sweater, a signet ring, or a shirt and tie, people were pigeonholed. All these externals didn't count any more when you couldn't see.

"That student is my best friend here," Ben answered testily. And because he could sense how Grandma was raising her eyebrows at his mother, he added even more snappishly, "And he's going to die in a few weeks."

Mornings, afternoons, evenings, and nights succeeded each other in a fixed pattern. But now the days didn't slip by any more. Too much had happened in ward three, too much that had touched Ben deeply.

In the first place, there were his talks with the student, who gave so intensely of himself to help

Ben at the beginning of his long road full of obstacles. Only once did he let slip why it was so important to him.

"I would so much like a bit of me to live on as something worthwhile in you."

Ben was fully able to put his mind at rest on that score.

Then there was his growing friendship with the odd, rough Jerry, who as well as a big mouth possessed a big, warm heart. It did one's soul good to see how he cosseted Ben.

"Nurse," he said one day to the rather strict nurse Ruth, "couldn't Bennie give me a push around for a bit? Then I'd have a chance to see something different from his orange lordship, the baker, and that hairy ape in the corner."

Nurse Ruth fetched a wheelchair and amid much laughter heaved Jerry into it.

"Go ahead and push, Ben. The lame leading the blind."

They had a lot of fun in the corridor, rolling along from one end to the other. Then Jerry said with a hint of mystery:

"Stop, Ben, and then go back a bit. To the right . . . a bit more. Yep, and now slowly and softly forward."

Ben pushed the chair forward carefully.

"A bit more to the left," hissed Jerry. What was he up to? They must be near the kitchen, thought Ben. He heard cups and saucers being stacked and the sound of running water. Then came the surprised voice of nurse Rose:

"Hello, what are you two doing here?"

"Push on, Ben, till you can't go any further."

Ben took two more steps.

"Ho! Stop!" cried nurse Rose with a giggle. Were they now all stuck in a corner?

"Shut your ears a minute, Ben," muttered Jerry huskily. "Rosie, come here a minute?"

"Not . . . no, Jerry, let me go!"

There was a shuffle of feet and a rustle of a stiff skirt. Then it seemed to Ben that nurse Rose lost her balance and fell into Jerry's lap.

"No, Jerry, you can't . . . " Nurse Rose's voice was smothered and it wasn't hard to imagine by what. There was a lengthy silence. Ben heard only the kettle bubbling on the stove. Then the chair shook under his right hand.

"So there," whispered Jerry, with a sigh of content. "That was my first, but it won't be my last."

Were they looking at each other? Was he kissing her again? Nervously Ben waited for nurse Rose to say or do something. Would she be mad and slap Jerry's face? Luckily that didn't happen.

"Oh, Jerry," she said softly, and her voice didn't sound angry. The opposite. Her feet touched the floor again. A stroking sound. Was she straightening her clothes?

"Rosie, in a year I'll be promoted. Will you come and sail with me on my ship?"

"You're mad!"

Jerry laughed, as carefree as a child.

"O.K., Ben, now reverse. Back to the corridor."

While he pushed the wheelchair back with one hand, Ben felt for the door with the other.

39

"No, dopey, more to the left," warned Jerry. Then he said even more warmly and persuasively:

"Rosie, it's a great life aboard."

In his imagination, Ben saw nurse Rose and Jerry leaning on a ship's rail watching the ocean.

"Don't forget, Bennie," muttered Jerry when they were back in the corridor, "you've heard nothing and seen nothing."

"Well, I certainly haven't seen anything." Ben grinned, and it was the first time he'd joked about his blindness. It gave him a feeling of satisfaction.

"Good for you, kid. Now roll back to the ward, and we'll tease his lordship for a bit."

Later, as he lay in bed listening to the radio, it occurred to Ben that both the student and Jerry had entrusted a very personal secret to him. And he asked himself, would they have done the same if he had been able to see . . . ?

At long last there came a morning that was completely filled by one simple sentence spoken by the doctor. He had taken off the bandage and looked at the nicely healing wounds. And then he said, "Well, Ben, as far as I'm concerned you may go home tomorrow."

*Go home.* The words zoomed joyfully through Ben's whole being. But a little later he had a sobering thought. How would he, how could he, break this news to the student?

# Chapter Four

WHEN his parents came to fetch him in a cab from the hospital, Ben's heart sank for a moment.

That difficult moment of parting had come. Good-bye to nurse Win, the other nurses, ward three. This gripped him harder and touched him deeper than he would have thought possible. Such a parting cut you through and through.

Nurse Win gave him a kiss and pressed the soft perfection of her unwrinkled cheek to his.

"Promise me, Ben, you'll hold your head high. When I've got a minute, I'll come and visit you."

Then good-bye to ward three, with the uncomfortable feeling that he was leaving real friends in the lurch. Without the least trouble Ben found his way to the beds and stretched out his hand first to the baker and then to his lordship.

"All the best. See you soon."

It was only when the phrase was out that Ben realized how silly it sounded.

Jerry, of course, had a joke or two ready on his lips. Only his last words were serious.

"Bennie, boy, I'm going to miss you. Who's going to wheel me to the kitchen when you're not here? Rose and I'll send you an invitation if it ever gets so far."

A shiver crept over Ben's back as he felt his way to the student's corner. He hadn't stayed in bed but was waiting for him by the door.

"Thanks . . . thanks for everything . . . "

Ben would have loved to say much more, but he couldn't get another word through his trembling lips.

Fortunately the student also kept it brief.

"Good-bye, Ben, keep on loving life. And make something of it."

Ben nodded.

"Courage, Ben!"

"You too! You too!"

Between his father and mother through the long passageways of the hospital to the main door. An ungainly tussle with the revolving doors, which rather upset his mother. Then to the waiting cab.

"Here we go," sang out his father.

"Yes, great, isn't it!" chimed in his mother.

The cab moved off. They drove round the first, now unseen, bend. The hospital—that waiting room in the midst of real life—already belonged to the past.

What a bewildering lot had happened in a few weeks. Ben now had the feeling that he'd said good-bye for good to the sporty, carefree boy he'd been. Not that he'd suddenly become adult, but a part of his youth was lost to him forever.

The ride home grew into a nightmare. It shocked Ben far more deeply than he had expected when they drove along familiar streets that he couldn't see. Sounds of now invisible traffic. Invisible people walking by. Invisible houses, stores, trees, and the invisible railway crossing.

"Where are we?"

"By the church."

The darkness, which in the small world of ward three had not seemed so overwhelmingly black, now enveloped Ben completely. For a moment he felt like a stowaway without a ticket for the journey through life. He clenched his teeth because he was dizzy from the cab's braking when he didn't expect it and from the swerving round bends he couldn't see.

"Where are we now?"

"We're just passing the delicatessen."

His mother and father tried to fill the blackness with small talk. That didn't help, of course. Weren't they taking home their blind child?

The cab slowed down.

"We're here," said Father. He laid his hand encouragingly on Ben's knee for a moment, then opened the door and got out to pay the driver.

Ben crawled out of the cab. Panicking for a second, he grabbed his mother's arm in fear and dismay.

Now he was standing in front of their own gate, with their own house behind it, and he saw none of it. Not a single image flashed on the screen of his thoughts, because his desperation hung like a pitch-black curtain in front of everything.

Home again, but all that was left of it was uncertain footsteps on the brick path through the lawn.

The door opened. The excited voice of Maryanne sailed through the air to meet him.

"Hi, Ben. Welcome home!"

He was given a clumsy kiss on his ear, because at the last minute he turned his head to the wrong side for it. Then he shuffled on through the utter darkness.

"Mind the step," warned his father. More words fit for a toddler that in the middle of his despair stung like wasps. Was it because of them that he lifted his foot too soon and so almost stumbled over that blasted brick step into the doorway?

Home again. Now he was standing in the hallway—in that once so familiar, now invisible, hallway —and it didn't bring him any joy.

"At last!" His mother's voice sounded gay and happy, because she could look after her own child again, no matter how mutilated he was.

"A cake's arrived," said Maryanne. "And Jeff rang to see if you were here yet. And Mrs. Maclean sent a box of candies. And Aunt Bessie . . . "

"All in good time," put in Dad, nervously thumbing at his lighter, which wouldn't light.

Hesitatingly Ben walked along the passage. His mother took his arm protectively, but he tugged himself free. The world under the bandage was ominously black.

"Are you tired? Would you like to lie down on the sofa?" Ben shook his head. He wanted to be alone. For God's sake, let him be alone for a minute with his panic and the lump in his throat.

"I'd like to go to my room for a while."

At last he felt the stair railing and the first treads. Mother followed him again.

"Can you manage?"

"Yes, Mom, I'll find it all right."

He said the words as affectionately as possible so as not to spoil completely the other's joy in his homecoming.

"Leave him alone for a bit." Whispered words from his father, who of course was making meaningful gestures to mother and Maryanne.

Halfway upstairs Ben stumbled on the last step before the landing. Happily, the rail gave him support in time.

Clumsily, defiantly, and half whimpering, he found his room.

Because he misjudged the distance, the door shut rather too hard and emphatically after him. Bang! Now that. Downstairs they'd be thinking that he was behaving like an ungrateful, spoiled, cowardly child. Well, let them think so.

Home again. Ben took a deep breath, then another and another. But it was some time before he managed to regain any composure.

The room smelled of paint. Had his father painted it while he'd been away? Carefully Ben began to feel the familiar walls. He sniffed the door. No, that hadn't had the benefit of the paintbrush.

His bed was still in the same place. But what was that?

"Hey!"

The table had been moved. Against the wall stood a

new chest, a brute of a thing, divided up into big and small cubbyholes. Had his parents made it and painted it?

Ben felt like bursting into tears when he realized how much thought and effort his parents had expended for his sake. A chest with cubbyholes. He'd be able to find his things easily, provided everything was put away in the proper place.

Now the table stood under the right-hand window. Ben walked around it and bumped into the chair. Clutching for support, his hand struck a heavy metal object on the table.

"What on earth . . . "

He felt a round knob, a cylinder, and round keys.

"A typewriter," he muttered to himself. His questing hands felt another object, and again his fingers landed on a keyboard. Another typewriter? Why two? Was his father getting extravagant?

Slowly the truth penetrated. He wouldn't be able to do his homework with a pen or pencil now. It would be unreadable for the teachers at his school. An ordinary typewriter solved that problem. Would the other machine with the much smaller keyboard perhaps produce braille letters?

"It's true!" Some sheets of paper lay on the left part of the table. His fingers recognized the tiny bumps of the dots of the relief writing pressed out of heavy paper.

The braille machine stood there as palpable evidence of the trouble taken by his parents. They had bought both machines after they had immersed themselves in the problems of their blinded son. He could bet his life that Mom had already put in a lot of practice on the braille machine.

Ben walked to the open window and took a big gulp of spring air. And it was as if the student's words drifted to him on the soft breeze.

"Ben, what really blinds and lames a human being is suspicion, fear, and rebelliousness. These bring darkness with them. But with a bit of faith, a bit of courage, and a bit of acceptance the light remains."

The student was right. During the oppressive journey home from ward three, darkness and hopelessness had completely mastered him. Now that the rebellious mood had abated, things began to fall into proportion again.

Ben put his head out of the open window. Through the bandage his eye sockets seemed to fill with the light of the sun. Beneath him was the yard. Familiar sights appeared in his imagination: the lawn, the gnarled currant bushes that would be in bloom now. Behind it the wall with his mother's roses and the brick path to the shed.

"Yes," said Ben aloud. The light was on his hands. He felt the sun on his face. From a high branch came the whistling of a blackbird.

It was good to be alive, and it was time to go downstairs.

He should finally let his parents know how fine it was to be home again.

"Home again, son," said his father, when they were seated at the table and delicious aromas were rising from roast beef, baked potatoes, and crisp green salad with lots of spring onions. The homecoming was to be celebrated with a feast. His nose had taken over from his eyes, because as he sniffed the odors Ben *saw* the dishes before him.

"Hungry?"

"Sure, Mom, dish it up."

"Jeff, will you help yourself to meat and pass the platter."

Mother had asked Peter and Jeff to eat with them— perhaps because she was anxious for it all to be like old times.

Ben had looked forward to having his friends there, but it wasn't turning out a success. It was difficult to say why. Their voices crisscrossed the table cheerfully, but their words reminded him of clothespins on a line without any wash to dry.

"You should have seen us on Saturday. Bob went in first because his father's on the committee . . . "

"That's the only reason. The nut lost us a great chance. It was all his fault that we lost."

They had lost badly three days before and it was still bothering them. A wrongly disallowed point. A referee who had missed something of the play. A foul that wasn't penalized. Baseball, baseball, baseball, as if the hospital had never existed. Once or twice Ben tried to tell them something about Jerry, his lordship, and the student. Peter and Jeff were willing listeners, but it didn't touch them. The least pause in the conversation, and it turned back to baseball.

"Say, did you see the game on Saturday on TV?" said Peter to Jeff.

"You bet! Fantastic!"

*Empty clothespins on the line*, thought Ben. For

48

the first time he felt a bit homesick for ward three and his talks with the student. That wasn't really fair. Before his accident hadn't he talked just as enthusiastically about baseball? And it had always been fun then.

No, it wasn't Peter and Jeff's fault. It was he who couldn't make the jump from the small world of the hospital to the baseball stadium.

"Ben, shall I help you?" asked his mother, when everyone's plate had obviously been filled.

"I can manage on my own. I did it in the hospital, though I made an awful mess."

"You can make as much mess as you like," said his father.

A silence followed—perhaps because Ben first missed his meat and put his empty fork to his mouth.

"How's school?" he asked quickly, realizing that they were now looking at him in some embarrassment.

"We're being killed with tests. Another two, for algebra and French."

"Stewart got a zero from Thomson because he sneaked a look at someone else's paper."

"I'll certainly never be able to do that in the future," said Ben, but nobody laughed, although he'd meant it as a joke. *No, the celebration wasn't a great success*, thought Ben as he poked at his meat, spilled his salad. His father and mother weren't to blame at all. They were trying their hardest to make it click. Why on earth didn't it?

Suddenly Ben realized that he had expected to be the center of attention, that he had, without meaning to, anticipated more sympathy. There was no point in sulking. He had to make that leap from ward three to the small world of home. Ben stabbed his baked potato with his fork and took a mouthful.

"Where are you playing Saturday?" he asked with his mouth full.

"Away, against Victoria," answered Peter. "It'll be rough. We've got to get to second place."

"I'll come and watch," said Ben, even if *watch* was not the right word.

"That'll be great," cried Jeff. "With you on the sideline we're bound to make it."

"I'll come and fetch you," promised Peter enthusiastically.

All at once the old familiar feeling was back. The conversation flowed: about baseball, school, girls, parties, and also about the hospital. All at once they couldn't find words enough; words like clothespins, now heavy with the clean, half clean, sometimes faded and tattered wash of everyone's life.

Even during that first day his parents realized that Ben wanted to be as independent as possible.

All parental aid and protectiveness was gently but decidedly waved away. "No, leave me alone," he'd say, or "I can manage on my own."

When Peter and Jeff had gone home and Ben went to bed, dog-tired but contented, his father and mother stayed behind in the living room, though rather reluctantly.

"We'll be up in a minute." It sounded relaxed, but Maryanne got an anxious nod to follow Ben and keep an eye on his progress.

Most children inhabit a wide, wonderful, internal world, of which only a tiny part is visible. They see and feel infinitely more than those around them realize.

Maryanne was like that. Chattering lightheartedly, she followed Ben up the stairs. Inside her she was keenly aware of what was going on in her brother's inner world.

"It was a good day, wasn't it?"

"Sure."

"Great that you're home."

"You can say that again."

Short sentences about nothing, but at the same time Maryanne put his pajamas ready to hand on the bed. She watched too that Ben didn't bump into anything or fall over the chair. Thanks to her, the washcloth, the toothbrush, and the towel seemed to find their own way into his hands. She had never felt so close to her brother. Was it because of that feeling that the talk became less casual? Hesitatingly, in the way brothers so often talk to sisters, Ben asked:

"How were Father and Mother when I was in hospital?"

And Maryanne, young as she was, knew exactly what he meant.

"They haven't had a quarrel since your accident."

"Truly?"

"Cross my heart."

Ben's hands slid along the new chest.

"Dad made that for you."

"Yes, I know."

More questions jostled in Ben's head, but they couldn't be answered yet.

"Do you know what's going to happen? Can I go back to high school? Or do I have to go to an institute for the blind?"

Maryanne shrugged her shoulders, but of course her brother couldn't see that and she answered quickly:

"I don't know about that."

"Have you heard anything?"

Maryanne hesitated, just for a second, then she decided to fib.

"No . . . "

She had to do that because no agreement had yet been reached in the family about that life-size question.

When his father and mother came to say good night, Ben was already in bed. Maryanne was given a nod to go to her own room.

"It's marvelous to have you home again," said his mother, tucking in the blanket.

"What's going to happen to me now?"

"The first job is to learn braille, Ben. In the beginning it will seem a hopeless task, but in time your fingers will read the letters just as your eyes did."

"Can I stay on at high school?"

So the all-important question had been put into words. Ben waited tensely for the reply. He had the feeling that the next words would decide his whole future.

"Maybe and maybe not," said his father carefully.

"We've still got to go into it thoroughly to find out what would be best for you."

"Have you spoken to the rector yet?"

"Yes." Again it was his father who answered. "He thought a blind student would be too heavy a burden for the teachers. He didn't know if the textbooks they use exist in braille. To be honest with you, he had a good number of objections."

"Oh . . . " Ben felt fear growing again. Then his mother spoke.

"Ben, you had an excellent report. We're going to work hard to make up for what you've missed these last weeks. And then we'll convince the rector that you wouldn't be a problem at school."

"I get it," mumbled Ben. "Most high schools don't want anyone handicapped. That's what you mean, isn't it?"

"We'll soon let them see that you're not handicapped," said his mother with great conviction.

Ben nodded. They were words after his own heart. All the same, just to make sure, he asked:

"I don't have to go to an institute?"

"Ben," said his father, his voice sounding very vulnerable, "you're just home. Most important of all is that you get strong and regain your old abilities. After that we'll find out together what will be best for you."

"First, we're going all out to get you back in your old class."

Ben felt his mother tucking him in while she spoke the words, something she hadn't done in years.

"Now go to sleep. It's been an exhausting day for you."

There came a good night kiss, as if he were the same age as Maryanne.

"It's been a great day," said Ben. "Thanks for everything."

His father and mother went downstairs. The living room door clicked shut. More clearly than ever Ben heard the sounds of the house: the creaking of the stairs, the wind rattling a window, the subdued hum of the icebox in the kitchen. A car passed through the night stillness of the street.

# Chapter Five

"I CAN'T do it! I can't!"

Cursing, Ben beat the table with his clenched fists. His clumsy, still-not-sensitive-enough fingers couldn't do the work of his eyes. That rotten typewriter had fifty keys and the letters were unbelievably haphazard: the *a* next to the *s*, the *c* next to the *v*.

His mother sat beside him. She had been a secretary and knew how to touch-type. Again and again she guided his fingertips over the keyboard.

"If I could only get a glimpse, just for a few seconds, of where the letters are," said Ben with despair in his voice.

"Be patient, please; it takes time."

Patient! But of course Mom was right. He had only started two days ago, and in such a short time you couldn't expect miracles.

"It's almost noon. That's enough for this morning," said his mother, pushing the typewriter to the back of the table. Ben stood up with a sigh. Already he could find his way downstairs much more easily than a few days before. His hand gripped the white stick that his parents had ordered together with the type-writer from the blind institute. It had its own place in the corner of the hall.

"Where are you going, Ben?"

"I'm just going to get a breath of fresh air."

"Oh . . . yes . . . do that."

She sounded rather hesitant but for once didn't tell him to be careful.

He opened the door and stepped outside. While he cautiously shuffled his way to the gate, he sensed that Mom was watching his progress from the kitchen window. Was she feeling sad as she watched him poke along? Would she call to him to stay in the yard and not yet venture onto the street?

Swinging his stick, Ben found the gate. Feeling like a real daredevil, he stepped through it and turned sharp right. That way he was quickest out of Mother's sight.

The stick slid along the edge of the sidewalk. Where was he planning to go? Yes, to the little park further up. There was a bench there that shouldn't be all that hard to find. He only had to walk on to the first corner and cross the street there.

In his thoughts it had all seemed so simple. But the reality was bitterly different. He stumbled. He bumped into the mailbox because he had forgotten it was there. Sweat poured off him. When he finally reached the corner, his legs were trembling and he felt hopelessly lost in the darkness.

Was he standing in the right place? Could he cross straight over or must he go more to the left?

A car shifted gears as it passed. Footsteps. Female heels clicked on the cement. Then a voice:

"Can I help you?"

"No, thank you. I can manage."

He had to do it on his own or he'd never learn. The heels clicked on and finally died away.

Ben decided to cross because the street seemed to be quiet now. Was he right? He's been foolish to refuse help. Why shouldn't people be allowed to help him?

"Now!"

He thrust out his stick and stepped off the sidewalk. A moment of panic. No, go on. If you hesitated in the middle of the street you were asking for trouble. Faint sounds of traffic. A car purred round the corner.

"Ouch . . . " He stumbled over the curb, but at least he had reached the other side. How infinitely more difficult and complicated it all was in reality than he had imagined in the hospital.

"Darn it!" He had walked into a hedge. Twigs scraped his face. Where was the park now? Left? Right? Again he was overcome by panic. With tiny steps and his right hand stretched out he timidly advanced. He heard the grinding sound of loose gravel under his feet.

"For Christ's sake!" Ben took a deep breath. The hedge came to an end. Was he now at the path into the park? Or was he at the entrance to some stranger's garden? Footsteps behind him. Yes, go on and ask. People were there to help each other.

"Hello?"

"Yes?" A man's hesitating voice.

"Am I at the park?"

"Uh . . . the park? No, not yet. That's a bit further on."

The man had a cleft palate, but he was a friendly soul. He took Ben's arm. "Do you want me to lead you there?"

"Thanks," said Ben. "I can't see anything. Once I get there I'll remember it."

It was fine to be able to stride out for a bit and let his muscles do their normal work. It really gave him a lift.

"Here it is. Can I do anything else for you?"

"Where's the bench?"

"To the right and to the right of the path. Do you want to go there?"

"I can find it myself. Thanks a lot."

"It's a pleasure."

Slowly Ben shuffled along the path, always probing ahead of him with the stick. As long as the gravel crunched under his feet he was in the right direction.

Bang! The stick struck metal. That must be the rubbish bin. He was nearly there. Yes, there it was. He had found the bench. Dead tired, but with a sigh of relief, Ben sank down on it.

The scent of blossom and dried fertilizer. The spring sun on his face. A bird whistled and Ben asked himself if he'd ever be able to distinguish all the varying birdsongs. Now it was such a dominating sound, while before he'd hardly been aware of it.

The gloom caused by the typewriter lifted. Ben felt

content and fulfilled. For the first time since his accident he had ventured onto the street and he had reached the place he chose under his own steam. Sure, there had been moments of panic and fear. It was no joke finding the way in absolute darkness. But here he was, sitting on the bench.

Ben smiled a broad smile. Perhaps it wouldn't have been quite so wide if he'd known that his mother had anxiously followed him at a safe distance.

The whine of traffic in the distance. The chirping of birds around him. The wind against his sweaty forehead, blowing some coolness under the sweltering bandage. Kindergarten was out, judging from the shouting and yelling. Then some children's voices close at hand.

"I want to be a pilot."

"I want to be the captain of a great big ship."

"What about you, Johnnie?"

"Me?" From his voice, Johnnie must be a child of about four.

"Yeah, you!"

"I'm going to be a king, of a whole country."

Laughter.

"Dopey! You can't. Your father would have to be a king, or your mother a queen, or you can't be king."

"Yes, I can," insisted Johnnie. "I'll get to be king by myself."

Ben could see the kids around him. Especially Johnnie—a sturdy little chap with a runny nose and a shoelace undone.

"How? How will you get to be king?" cried the others.

59

"Well, first I'll buy a horse, and then I'll slay the dragon."

"Ha, ha! A dragon! There are no dragons!"

"Then I'll slay something else," said Johnnie quickly. "And then I'll free the princess, and then I'll marry her. And then her father'll die. And then the princess will be queen, and then," he cried in triumph, "I'll be king."

"Ha, ha! Where'll you find a princess?"

"Somewhere," said Johnnie, full of conviction. There was silence for a moment. Ben could hear them thinking.

"And what if the princess doesn't love you? What if she won't marry you?"

"Yeah, Johnnie, what'll you do then?"

"Then I'll be the queen's gardener," said Johnnie in a flash.

"But a gardener can't be king."

"Oh, yes, he can," snapped Johnnie. "Because the queen will say, 'John, I'm tired. I don't want to be queen any longer. All that bother. Someone else will just have to worry for me!' "

"Then what?"

"Then she'll say to me, 'John, you're the best gardener in my kingdom. You'll be the best king, too.' And so I'll be a king after all."

The words obviously made an impression, because again there was a short silence.

"And then I'll be the boss," said Johnnie triumphantly. "And I won't have to answer any more questions. A king doesn't have to."

Was he walking away? Yes. Ben heard his footsteps approaching over the gravel. Johnnie the king.

"You can't be a king," called another youngster after him.

"Yes, I can," shouted the little king with utter confidence.

Ben stood up with a grin. The children's voices had done him a world of good. If you had as strong a faith as Johnnie's in the future, you pushed yourself through all sorts of difficulties.

The other kids now strolled past him.

"Hey, will you do me a favor? Take me across the street, please."

"Have you hurt your eyes?"

"Looks like it, doesn't it?"

"Can't you see anything?"

"No," said Ben. "I can't see anything."

"Nothing at all?"

"Nothing at all. Not you kids. Not the houses. And not the street."

"What do you see then?"

"Other things."

"But what?"

"I see Johnnie sitting on a splendid throne with a golden crown on his head."

To that they had no answer. Ben couldn't see their wondering faces, but he felt two small hands gripping his. They led him—pointing out every crack in the road—with the utmost care to the other side.

Only when he pushed open the gate to his house—it was easy to find because of the overhanging pine—

did his mother, who had followed him at a discreet distance, come to meet him.

"I was just coming to fetch you," she said, and Ben was reassured to hear how relaxed her voice sounded. Clearly she hadn't had a moment of uneasiness.

"What's the time, then?" In the future he'd better pay more attention to the chime of the church clock.

"Nearly twelve thirty," said his mother. "I don't want lunch to be too late, because the doctor's coming and that could be early in the afternoon. Have you had a nice walk?"

"Yes," answered Ben. "It was great." And with some pride he added, "I walked to the bench in the park."

"All that way?"

His mother's voice sounded amazed; for the sake of her child's happiness she could certainly pretend a bit.

After lunch Ben worked on the braille alphabet. Thanks to his mother's help, he could already project many of the letters on the screen in his brain. He thought gratefully of Louis Braille, the blind Frenchman who a century and a half ago had made it possible for blind people to read, write, and count. For the first time in his life, Ben appreciated the great advantage it was that he could learn easily and had an excellent memory. But it was depressing that his fingertips still blocked the message between the paper and his brain. Was it a question of practice and patience? The doctor still hadn't come. Was it already three o'clock? Half past? It was a darned nuisance to have to keep asking Mom the time. He wondered if braille watches existed.

Ben pushed back his chair, stood up, and went toward the door. His hand banged against the washbasin and he froze on the spot. Now the mirror was in front of him. He bent his head forward a bit. In his thoughts he first saw his face as it used to be. Then came the thick bandage and he could imagine how he had looked then. And now there was the smaller bandage fixed with tape. What would appear if that bandage was removed today?

Ben stood motionless before the glass. He did his best to imagine how he would look from now on. First of all he saw dark holes where his eyes had been. Would they be covered with misshapen, drooping eyelids and under them a weird strip of white?

"Oh, God." Fear overcame him that he would be unbearable to look at. That people would be repulsed. And, above all, that no girl would ever look at him. Wouldn't that be the worst of all? Of course, he could wear dark glasses. But dark glasses coupled with a white stick made him think of the pathetic old blind beggars he'd seen shuffling along busy shopping streets.

"Don't let it wreck you," the student had said. The student. Now that he thought of him, Ben felt a little ashamed. What were ugly eyelids compared with waiting for death?

Ben sighed. Come what might, he'd have to accept it. There was no other way.

The front door opened and closed again.

"He's upstairs. Will you come with me?" Mother's voice downstairs and then firm footsteps in the hall.

The doctor had come.

Ben shook off a shiver of nerves. In a few minutes the bandage would come off, and what was under it was there forever. And forever was darned long.

Footsteps on the stairs. A pause on the landing and Mother's whispered voice. The door of the room opened.

"Hi, Ben."

"Hullo, doctor."

"You look good. Got some color in your cheeks again."

"Can the bandage come off today?"

"We'll have a look."

The bag was set down on the table. Water running as the doctor washed his hands at the basin.

"I'll fetch a clean towel." Mother went out of the room and came back again.

"Here you are."

"Thanks."

Ben swallowed hard. Now it had to happen. The doctor opened his bag. Instruments were put on the table.

What a long time it took. It was like a movie in slow motion. The cork was taken from a bottle of strong-smelling stuff.

"Sit down here a minute."

The chair was pushed to the window. Mom pushed him gently toward it.

"Put your head further back, Ben. Yes, like that."

The doctor's cool hand on his face. A wet wad over

the plaster. A sickly smell in the room. Yes, now the fingers were pulling the bandage loose. The eyebrow hairs held fast and he felt a twinge of pain.

"Hm," muttered the doctor.

That could mean anything and Ben held his breath. He must listen for his mother's reaction. If she should cry out or say something with a tremor in her voice, it would mean that he was badly mutilated. Was she still standing behind him? Had she seen nothing?

"Hm."

Cool fingers pulled up the right eyebrow. Ben could keep silent no longer.

"Well?" In that one short word lay long weeks of fear.

"The wounds have healed nicely."

Mother moved. Ben felt her nervous hand on his shoulder as she bent over him. And then her voice.

"Oh, yes."

Only two words, but they sounded relieved.

"How does it look?"

"Very good, Ben," said the doctor. "I'm pleased. The scars are still a bit fiery, but that will fade in time."

"Am I . . . is it . . . do I look horrible?"

"Of course not," said the doctor, putting his things together.

"Really not, Mom?" Almost painfully Ben sought for complete certainty.

"No, really not." Mother had to fight against tears that came because she'd never see her son's eyes again.

She bit her lip. "It's not at all horrible."

"How then? Exactly how does my face look?"

"Well, you look like someone with his eyes closed. Quite ordinary."

"Not . . . repulsive?"

"Certainly not," the doctor laughed. "You didn't think we had bunglers in the hospital, did you?"

"No, not that, but . . . "

"Believe me, Ben, the wounds are beautifully healed and after a while there'll be nothing to see."

"I don't have to wear dark glasses?"

"Not at all."

"Thank God for that," Ben whispered, and all the cramping tension made way for a feeling of elation and gratitude. Now that the bandage was off he felt as if he'd been given back his face.

# Chapter Six

WHEN you're blind, the words you hear count double. Ben had first experienced that in the hospital when nurse Annie had come to help him instead of nurse Win. What a difference their voices had made!

Since then, words and voices had grown more and more significant. For, after all, didn't they reflect everyone's personality, character, and soul?

When anyone talked to him, Ben no longer saw a face, no laughing or embittered mouth, no busily waving hands elaborating people's words. Now he had to do without the appearance, without knowing if someone were looking skeptical or shy or defiant. It was a great lack. But Ben had discovered that he could give people a form all the same by listening attentively to their voices. There were vain, aggressive, and boastful voices; tired, melancholy, almost inaudible voices; and voices that sounded discontent. There were voices that threw out words and voices that were thoughtful, voices full of feeling, full of plain dullness, sometimes full of jealousy. A small word like *yes* grew to have lots of nuances: there was a joyful *yes*, a fearful *yes*, a businesslike *yes*, a hesitating *yes*, a courageous *yes*.

Not the external but the inner world grew in range, in which words because of their tone became accurate messengers telling about the nature of each person. Ben was to realize that once more on Saturday afternoon when he went with Peter and Jeff to the baseball stadium to "watch" the match with Victoria.

"What's the time now?" Ben asked for the third time in half an hour.

"Quarter after one," said Dad.

"Could they have forgotten?"

"Of course not. They'll be here in a minute."

Ben lounged around the house waiting for his friends. He felt nervous and he couldn't say why. Was he afraid to meet the boys on his old team? Afraid, because now blind Bennie would not be able to play? Afraid, in case like a bird that lost its course he might land in an alien environment?

Rattle on the street. It was Peter's mudguard, which had been loose long before the accident. Was Jeff there, too?

"Hi, Ben."

"Hullo, Bennie."

The bikes halted.

"Gee, Jeff," called Maryanne. Her voice sounded excited. "What's that you've . . . "

Ben couldn't see that both Peter and Jeff had put their fingers to their lips with a *sh* gesture. Maryanne swallowed the rest of her question.

"Hurry up, Ben," said Peter impatiently. "We're a bit late already."

Ben moved forward uncertainly, feeling for the bike with his stick.

"Yeah, come on. I'm here." It sounded a bit offhand and abrupt. "Up boy, climb on behind."

Father and Mother looked on in astonishment. They were taken aback that Peter and Jeff were treating their son as if he still had both eyes, as if nothing were changed, as if his going with them to the baseball stadium were perfectly normal.

"Have fun," called Mom cheerfully, but her heart bled to see Ben perch there so vulnerably and at one point almost lose his balance.

"See that you win," yelled Father after them, with a deep wistfulness inside because he'd never again watch his son playing a game.

"We'll teach them a lesson," promised Jeff.

"Ben, hold on to my bag," said Peter.

Off they went, mudguard rattling, making a rather unsteady course toward the Victoria stadium.

Peter and Jeff put their bikes in the shed. They walked along the cement path to the clubhouse. There was a hum of voices all around them.

"I'll wait here," Ben said. He was aware that glances were being thrown at him from all directions. The pitch, the spectators, the players—everything seemed to be gripping him by the throat. And because he was so tense, the darkness in his head was utterly black.

"I'll stay here."

69

"Are you crazy?" exclaimed Jeff. He gripped Ben's arm more firmly. "You're coming to the locker room with us. Everyone wants to see you again."

"No, pal."

"Yes, pal."

He let himself be taken. Although he should have known from the sounds that they were nearly there, he managed to stumble over the step.

"Watch out for the doorstep," warned Peter, too late.

"Yeah!"

And there was the smell, that typical locker room smell of sweat, grubby gear, and unwashed shirts. From all sides enthusiastic, warm voices greeted him:

"Hi, Ben!"

"Great to see you!"

Claps on his shoulder. Grips on his arm. More often than not his right hand clasped by two hands at once. All the warmth made Ben relax instantly. His head became clearer inside and he could imagine the locker room and the boys around him. It was no longer so difficult to recognize their voices:

"Hi, Dickie!"

"Hello, George, mind you keep them running."

"Hi, Jimmy."

"Great that you've come to see us," Jimmy said eagerly.

Ben was given a place on the bench. He heard the sound of bare feet on the floor, rummaging in bags, shoes tossed into lockers. And talk about the coming match, homework, a party to which some of them were invited. As usual, the loud voice of Charlie sounded over all the others, a voice filled with dare-deviltry and recklessness. Voices demanding attention and voices trying to be funny. They hurt Ben's ears. Had he become too used to the calmer, gentler, and more spacious world of ward three? The little world of the locker room seemed crowded and hectic.

A whistle sounded outside. There was a thump of feet toward the field.

"Coming?" said Jeff.

"My stick." Ben gripped it firmly, held it out, and this time felt the doorstep in time. All the same, he nearly lost his balance in the rush of players going out.

"Hey, can't you watch where you're going?" called a boy from Victoria who saw the white stick too late.

They walked to the stand. The sun had come out. Ben felt its warmth on his face.

"Put me on the side, Jeff. In the sun, if you can."

"O.K. This way." *Like a horse on a leading rein,* thought Ben, feeling the pressure of Jeff's hand on his shoulder. Running footsteps on the springy ground. The dull bounce of a ball. The voice of Harry's father, the coach, rounding up his team.

"Wait a minute," said Jeff.

Ben halted obediently. Then he noticed that a number of the boys were gathered round him. Was Harry's father going to give them his usual preplay pep talk? "Charlie, watch the outside men. George, no fooling around. Bennie, remember to play it wide."

"Come on then, Dickie," said Harry's father. At once there was silence except for the gusty spring wind.

71

"Well, Ben," began Dickie in a rather awkward voice. *For heaven's sake,* thought Ben. Despairingly he clenched the stick between his fingers, because he felt a speech coming. If he'd only known.

"Ben, it's marvelous that you came today. We've all of us missed you not only as top scorer but as a friend."

"But, Dickie . . . " Ben tried to stop the flow, but Dickie went on indefatigably.

"Remember that it was you who really won that last match for us with that beaut of a hit. You said then, 'It was pure luck. I hit it with my eyes shut.' We've often thought of these words since. With your eyes shut! But even if you can't score any more in baseball, we're all quite sure that your score in life will be very high."

Ben felt like sinking into the ground by now. Again and again he poked the grass with his stick, not knowing what to do for embarrassment.

"We wanted to give you something from the team, Ben, not a farewell gift, because you still belong." And then, in a different tone, "Hey, Pete, give it a ring."

A bicycle bell tinkled.

"It's a tandem," said Dickie, and with that, thank the Lord, the worst was over. "Ben, in case you were thinking that you could plunk your behind on one of our luggage racks every week, we thought, *if we buy him a tandem he'll have to do some peddling himself.* And as far as the front seat goes, you can always count on one of us."

Ben swallowed and swallowed again. Had his stay in the hospital made him so sensitive? Then Jeff drew him forward and guided his hands to the handlebars.

"How about that? It's painted white and red, the club's colors."

Ben knew he had to say something, but he couldn't find words right away. And how could he speak with that lump in his throat?

"Thanks, all of you. Thanks a lot. This, this is just too much. So get out there . . . and give Victoria a hiding."

And he whispered to Jeff, who was still standing next to him, "For goodness sake, take me someplace quiet."

Jeff's hand came down again on his shoulder. He was gently propelled to a quiet, sunny spot on the side. There he collapsed, like a wild creature returning to its safe lair after wandering in the dark woods.

He felt limp from all the emotion.

Ben had never realized how much and how loudly their team shouted during a match. The yells crisscrossed the plate.

"Over here! Here!"

"Give it up, Georgie!"

"Wide and easy!"

"You goofball, quit fooling!"

From all the shouting he could deduce where each player was. And by the running feet and the bounce of the ball, Ben could make out more or less how the game was going.

"I'll get it!"

"No, Harry, it's for me."

Ben could see Dickie racing forward and Harry

73

watching tensely. Yelling players, out for victory and with eyes only for the ball. Didn't their excitement seem a bit silly if you thought of nurse Win, of Jerry, of the dying student? All the same, it was great of them to give him a tandem bike. The warmth that it had kindled inside Ben was still glowing.

"Come on, boys, get on with it," he yelled over the pitch.

Ten minutes' play had passed. Ben was so engrossed that he didn't hear soft footsteps approach. It was only when he heard a cough that he realized someone was standing beside him.

"Hello, Ben."

Quite unnecessarily, Ben turned his head. He hadn't recognized the voice.

"Hullo . . . " He didn't commit himself further.

"It's Theo. Theo Ballantine."

"You here?" Ben heard the surprise in his own voice. What was Theo, an elusive figure from school, a wizard in class, but a timid, clumsy lump in gym— what was Theo doing at a baseball match?

"I heard you'd be here this afternoon."

"Yeah."

Ben had trouble recalling Theo's face clearly. He'd always kept apart from the others. Or had the others not bothered about him, because . . . yes, why?

"How's it going?" asked Theo in his deliberate voice. Not that he cared two pins.

"Not much scoring."

"Oh."

What were they to talk about? Ben thought he'd

better ask something about school, but Theo got in before him.

"I wanted to write to you. I didn't, so that's why I'm here. I wanted to tell you, well, not only that I'm darned sorry about the accident. Everyone is, of course."

Bellowing on the field. The whistle of the referee and a reprimand for someone. But Ben's attention was no longer on the game. Now he was listening intently to the careful, thoughtful voice of Theo, in which the slowness and dullness seemed to have taken on new color.

"If you'd like it, I'd be glad to help you with the classwork."

"Gosh." Again Ben was at a loss for words.

"You've fallen behind because of the accident, but we could soon make it up. Then you won't have to repeat. You'll be able to stay in our class."

"I don't think the rector will think much of that."

"Why not?"

"Someone blind, like me, is just a nuisance in a class."

"I don't see that," said Theo. "Honestly, I've thought about it a lot. We can deal with all the problems. That's why I'm here, you see. To tell you that. If you like, I'll come every day and help you. I've enough time."

"That's really nice of you."

"Think about it."

That slow voice. In the dark world behind Ben's closed eyes that voice reflected another boy than the withdrawn, colorless Theo he'd actually seen in class. Was it possible, thought Ben, now that he was blind he'd discovered the real Theo? His team had given him a tandem bike, and he sure could use it. But Theo had given himself.

Loud cheers on the pitch.

"Peter made a great catch."

"That's fine. We'll win today."

And they did. Shouts of joy after a period of tense silence were proof enough of that.

With his team winning, with his red-and-white tandem in the club colors, with a newly discovered friend sitting beside him, Ben thought gratefully that it was his best day since the accident. In spite of being blind, he felt very satisfied with life.

# Chapter Seven

"DURING three days of battle the Roman legions were destroyed in the Teutoburg Forest by rebellious Germanic tribes. Of the 30,000 men only a handful of veterans survived to bring news of the disaster to the fortresses and encampments along the Rhine . . . "

Theo's voice broke off.

"That uprising in Germany was in the year 9 A.D., wasn't it?" asked Ben.

"That's right. Will I read that bit over again?"

"You don't have to," said Ben. "I've got it now."

That was true. Now that he was blind, history—that lesson taught by the dead to the living—spoke much more clearly to him than before. While Theo was reading aloud, Ben had clearly seen before him Arminius's revolt against the Romans. Leading the legions was the noble Varus, proud and erect on his purebred stallion. Behind him stretched the long marching column, the wagons with tents, weapons, provisions, finding its way with difficulty in the inhospitable marshes. The young officers rapping out commands to the cohorts. The curses of the old centurions. And then, all at once, the attack in the rear by the Germans. Their whizzing arrows and their barbarian battle song. Like a film, the pictures from the past flashed through Ben's thoughts.

"We're getting on fast," said Theo with satisfaction. "A few more times and you'll have caught up with us in history."

"You're helping me tremendously."

"I'm enjoying it, you realize that?"

"If only all your bother isn't going to be for nothing."

His father still had to have a talk with the rector, but he wanted to wait a while until Ben had a good grip on his work again and could clearly show that he could keep up with the class.

"Like to bet that you'll be back with us in September?"

"I hope so," said Ben, but he didn't feel at all sure about it.

At home the days had long acquired a set pattern. Ben kept rigidly to the schedule he'd arranged with his father and mother.

In the morning he began to practice the braille alphabet. After an hour his mother joined him. She had been hard at work with all sorts of textbooks and was trying to help Ben to the best of her ability. After a break for coffee, the practicing was continued on the typewriter. There were good moments and there were bad. Sometimes Ben stormed to his feet, shouting that he couldn't do it. Then sometimes his fingertips seemed to gain in sensitivity, and he received the braille signs and found the keys better.

"Ben, you've typed the last four letters correctly," his mother could then say with pleasure, although her patience was stretched to the utmost. "Now do you see that your fingers are beginning to find their way among the keys?"

Ben didn't see it. His despair sometimes made his mother reproach herself that she wasn't teaching him properly. Usually he immediately regretted his behavior. "Sorry, sorry, I didn't mean it like that," he would say, and to give his mother some satisfaction in return for all her patience, he'd set to work with extra vigor. And so they staggered on, fighting to overcome problems that seemed hopeless.

A half hour before noon, Ben always took a stroll. Now he could find his way to the bench in the park without much trouble. Often he went and sat there until the kindergarten came out. Then the park was filled with voices. Shrieking voices. Excited voices. Shy voices. And voices that made the impossible possible. It was a source of inspiration to Ben to listen to their childish fantasies.

There they came again, those voices filled with derring-do. Ben sat motionless on the bench, his ears riveted.

"My father is so strong he can stop a train!"

The voice of Billy, who was always reaching for the heights.

"And my father's so rich he can buy a whole train."

That was the voice of Johnnie, who was to become king of a whole country.

"If your father buys a train, my father will stop it. Then the train'll be no good to your father."

"Then my father'll buy two trains," decided Johnnie at once.

"My father can *easily* stop two trains."

"Then my father'll buy three. If your father stops the two trains, we'll ride away in the third one."

"Then my father'll put his foot out and stop it."

"He can't do that," crowed Johnnie. "He's only got two feet and my father's got three trains."

"Oh, yes, he can," said Billy with utter conviction. "He'll stop two trains with his feet and the third one with his little finger."

There was a momentary silence. Now it was getting difficult.

"What if my father buys ten trains?" Johnnie tried cautiously.

"Then my father'll stop all of them. One with each finger."

"And then my father'll buy a plane," shouted Johnnie, once more on the attack. "He's got loads of money!"

"But my father'll pull that plane out of the sky!"

"He can't! He can't! Because he's only got ten fingers and they're all holding trains."

Johnnie's triumph seemed to be total.

"Oh, yes, he can," said Billy slowly. You could sense that he was still busy thinking.

"How, then?"

"With his teeth," said Billy. "He'll just bite that plane out of the sky. He's strong enough."

Johnnie, still not beaten, had his answer ready:

"Then my father'll buy a steamship and sail away over the sea."

"Then my father will throw the ten trains into the harbor and your father won't be able to get out."

"Yes, he will!"

"No, he won't!"

"You're a big bragger!"

"Whatever you say, that's what you are!"

They came up to the bench, still scolding and arguing, and stopped.

"Hello, Ben." Trains and planes were forgotten.

"Hello."

"Shall we take you across the road?"

"Thanks," said Ben.

A sweaty paw and a cool one took his hands. Slowly they made their way along the path.

"My granny's deaf. That's awful, too," said Billy.

"And I've got an aunt who has to sit in a chair with wheels because she can't walk. That's much awfuller," Johnnie at once announced. Were they going to begin all over again?

"If you're crazy, that's even more awful," cried Billy.

"My grandpa's dead. That's the worst of all." Johnnie's voice was brimming over with joy, because he had finally triumphed over Billy with a dead grandfather.

"You're there, Ben."

"Yes, I feel it. Thanks a lot." Ben tapped against the edge of the sidewalk, for him an accurate beacon showing him the way home. Behind him the voices of Billy and Johnnie faded away into the distance:

"Shall we see who can walk farthest with his eyes shut?"

"Oh, no!"

"Why not?"

"If you keep on walking with your eyes shut, maybe you'll land up in Russia. Or Canada."

"No, you won't."

"Yes, you will."

"No, you won't."

Ben grinned as he tapped his way home along the sidewalk.

A schedule had also been drawn up for the afternoons. After lunch, Ben worked for another hour with his mother until Theo came and all attention was focused on work for school. And then there were the evenings, when he slogged on with Dad after dinner until the news on television at eight o'clock.

"Where there's a will there's a way," Dad had said when Ben was just out of the hospital and they were talking about a work schedule. Mother had protested.

"You're taking on too much."

"Hard work never killed anyone."

"Yes, but . . . "

"If Ben wants to achieve something he'll have to

fight harder for it than other people. It's best if he begins right away."

His father wanted to keep on seeing him as a normal boy. And that was good. Or was he unable to accept his son's blindness and its consequences?

"Yes, but ... "

"Dad's right," Ben had intervened then. "For heaven's sake, what else have I got to do with all my free time?"

It was a case of falling and getting up again, of persevering until you felt like howling. But it was the only way, and he had to go on.

Ben went back one more time to the baseball ground. He wanted to be there when the last game of the competition was played.

It wasn't easy to find someone for the front seat. Peter had to go straight home after the match. Jeff had to go away with his parents. George had an hour of tutoring. At last, after many telephone calls, he found Jimmie willing to come and fetch him.

Again Ben sat in the locker room among his old friends. They were friendly enough; he couldn't say otherwise. Yet he had a feeling, which grew stronger and stronger, that the baseball stadium could no longer be his little world. Why did he have that feeling? Was it because of the conversation going on around him?

"Shall we go to a movie tonight?" The voice of Dick speaking to Jimmie. The film was a James Bond, which some of them had already seen.

"It's tomorrow that the big tennis tournament starts."

"Are you going to watch?"

"I think so."

"I'm not. I'm going to watch football."

All those voices belonged to a former world, thought Ben. All sorts of phrases that had formerly filled him with anticipation now slid past him.

"Dad's taking me to the boat show tomorrow." The voice of Charlie to Harry. "If you want to come along, give me a call."

James Bond, tennis, football, the boat show—that was all fine and thrilling if you had eyes to see. During the match Ben stood, feeling a bit lost, on the sideline. The shouting on the field was as loud and heated as last time.

"You're too far away," called Dick from the middle of the pitch. The words seemed to cut into Ben. Wasn't he standing too far away from all the others? Wasn't that the feeling he had had in the locker room? Wishing with all his heart he could join in with the others?

"I'm standing here like a mascot," he mumbled to himself. "That's all I'm good for."

Everyone has to find where he belongs. There's no work for a roadmaker at sea. And a blind Ben seemed completely superfluous in a baseball stadium.

However painful it was to admit that, it gave him a sense of relief because at the same time he could think of other areas where he'd never feel out of things.

"Come on, boys, give them all you've got," he

84

shouted out. It was a kind of farewell cry to his old team, who had given him a tandem and who had been close to him. Now he knew it for sure: the world of the baseball players could never be his.

Only later, much later, did Ben realize what had happened to him in that quarter of an hour on the sideline. As the other boys went on playing, he redirected his life from all that is physical and visible to all that is spiritual and essential in human existence. Although it was almost an unconscious process, he was slightly aware of it, because what his father had said to him some time after the accident flashed through his mind.

"You know, Ben, our eyes often distract us . . . "

As these words came into his head, there was a shout of jubilation from the players. A home run had given his old team the lead before the end of the inning.

The world in which he need never feel an outsider and which he now approached more deliberately was the world of books and conversation, of thinking and music. It was a world that was made fuller by Theo. The silent, shy Theo had turned out to be quite different than Ben had realized. It was amazing how much he knew, how much he had read and thought about. He came every afternoon around two. Beforehand he had worked out in detail the work he and Ben were to do.

"First of all, we'll do the Latin vocabulary," he would say firmly, "and then we'll go on to French."

He would chant the Latin and French words out

with a sort of angry patience and read out all the texts, sometimes two or three times.

"We ought to have a tape recorder," he said one afternoon when he'd read through a difficult piece of biology. "It would save us a lot of time."

"Sure, but these machines are darned expensive," Ben had replied.

"We're going to buy one all the same."

"*What?*"

"I've seen a really good one that we can buy on the installment plan."

"But, Theo, my parents have gone to so much expense already. I can't ask them for that. Really not."

"We can earn the money ourselves, can't we?"

"Earn it? And how can I do that?"

"We'll take on a paper route. Before I came today, I called. They can use another delivery boy. If we do it on the tandem it'll be far quicker."

Theo's voice, usually so slow, was full of excited anticipation. Suddenly Ben realized that he wasn't the only one who had entered a new world because of his blindness. It had also liberated the silent, withdrawn Theo from his loneliness and brought him human adventure beyond his dreams.

Slowly and inexorably the faces of his father and mother, of Maryanne, of his friends and acquaintances began to grow vague to Ben. Sometimes they slipped elusively into the gray mists behind his closed eyelids. To begin with, it made him sad, but he got used to it. People's outward appearance was no longer relevant. Neither long nor short hair, nor style of dress, nor jewelry could help him discover anything about the people he met. Something else gradually filled up that lack, and it was perhaps just as valuable. It couldn't be expressed in words or images because it had to do with the soul. Ben became more conscious of that when he did the paper route with Theo for the first time. At one house, Theo couldn't find the letter box so he rang the bell. An unknown woman opened the door and talked to them for a minute or two. In those few minutes Ben formed a clear picture of her.

"What a sad woman!"

"What makes you think that?" Theo asked in astonishment.

"I can hear it in her voice."

"But she didn't look at all sad. She looked very nice, too."

"Like to bet?"

Sure enough, the next day they heard that the woman's husband had died and that she couldn't come to terms with her solitary existence.

"How could you tell that about someone you'd never seen?"

Ben had to consider before he answered.

"Since I've been blind, meeting people is like hearing good or bad music. You can't see music, not even you. But the sounds seem to get inside you and they call up all sorts of feelings and thoughts. With me it happens with people. Although I can't see them, their voices penetrate and then . . . then I feel how they are."

"Did you feel that before?"

Ben shook his head.

"But why does it happen now?"

"You're distracted by everything you see. By dirty nails or a ragged shirt. Or restless eyes. Or . . . or a laughing mouth. Maybe you only looked at that woman's nice dress, or at an antique clock in the passage, or something like that. For me, all that doesn't count any more. I've got to go by what sounds in a voice. And in every voice there is always an echo of the soul."

It wasn't only that. Now that he was blind, Ben began to discover that people were far more vulnerable than he had thought. Everyone seemed to put up a sort of screen to hide his true feelings. There was often a wilderness of loneliness, sorrow, jealousy, or fear behind friendly, cheerful faces.

Before, all that had slipped past him unawares. Now that he was blind, Ben came to the realization that his insight into people was growing, and from time to time he played with the thought that he might well become a psychologist like the student. Yes, some good could certainly come out of trouble. But blindness had its frustrating and depressing aspects. Ben was to come across them, too.

# Chapter Eight

A S EACH person grows up—and after he is grown up, too—he has to travel along a path full of deep pitfalls. And because life consists of falling down and clambering up again, from time to time everyone finds himself in a deep pit. That's usually where he begins to fight against himself, or sometimes against circumstances, or the whole world, or even against God. These pits are isolated places with no view out. A person can be as trapped there as a wild bird fluttering back and forth along the wire netting of a cage and never finding a way to freedom.

Ben kept on falling into that sort of pit. Especially on the days when work didn't flow smoothly, black melancholy filled him. Then his blindness enveloped him. Life didn't seem to have any promise.

"Damn, damn, damn!" he would yell when he couldn't find the right keys of the typewriter under his mother's guidance. And he longed so intensely to see the letters in reality, even if only for a moment.

He learned by experience that it was those very

black moods—in which not only his frustration overcame him, but the whole world with its burden of strife and distress—that blinded Ben most. In such a frame of mind he bumped into objects and stumbled over doorsteps, and his fingers wouldn't pick out a single braille letter. Bungling around and cursing inside, Ben somehow got through such disheartening days. On those days the words he'd cried out to nurse Win seemed to ring true again: "My life, my whole life's ruined!"

But, like most people, Ben was tough. Over and over again he found the strength to climb out of those pits and then he realized again that the more he relaxed, the more cheerfully he accepted his lot, the better he could see in his thoughts the world around him.

"I jump from one dead end to another," he said to his father one evening. They had been sitting in front of the typewriter for about an hour, and it hadn't done a bit of good.

"That's inevitable," his father answered. "But just wait, you'll gradually be able to see ahead."

Two days later Ben fell into such a deep pit of gloom that he wondered if there was any point to going on living.

"Huh?"

Ben awoke with a start and sat up. For a second he was surprised not to see the curtains and the windowpanes shimmering in the light from the street lamps. Then he remembered—blind!

He had dreamed again about the snakes, which sometimes happened when he thought that life was letting him down. From the sounds, he deduced that it must still be night. The stair creaked, which you never heard in the daytime, and there was no traffic noise in the street. Was it one o'clock? Three o'clock? Or was the sun rising?

To shake off the hot clamminess of his dream, Ben pushed back the blankets and slung his legs out of bed. In his dream he had managed to keep on escaping from the black, squirming snakes. Now it was as if one of them had still managed to reach him and had twisted itself around his throat.

"Oh, God!"

Bitterly he struck his forehead with his fists, as if he were trying to force away the darkness from his eyes. For a moment he almost lost control. Then he stood up, hitching his pajama pants higher. Carefully he shuffled to the washbasin to wash the sweaty fear from his face with cold water. His hands found the chair and then touched the door, which stood ajar. Only then did he hear faintly his father and mother talking in their bedroom. Was it morning after all? Or was it still early in the night?

"Go and listen," said a compelling voice inside him. Why should he?

Because a talk in the night between his father and mother must be important. Because undoubtedly it would be about his being blind.

Ben tiptoed into the hall. He wasn't in the habit of eavesdropping, but his blindness had made him suspicious in some ways. He was really looking for reassurance because inside him too much was still wobbly and insecure.

The voices of his parents were intelligible in spite of the closed door. By turns they sounded firm and then brittle and anxious.

"I don't understand it. The rector is such a nice, humane kind of man." Mother's voice, positive and sharp.

"He is. Honestly, during a teachers' meeting they went into every possibility for Ben. And the verdict was negative in the end." That was Dad's voice, sad and shaken.

Ben saw his father and mother before him, sitting up in bed and lighting one cigarette after another.

"And now what?"

"I told you already. The rector thought an institute for the blind was the best solution."

"No, never that."

"But if they all think that, unanimously. They've far more experience than we have, haven't they?"

"No, over my dead body."

Deeply shocked, Ben clung to the stair railing. His whole body shook with helplessness and rage. After two weeks of wrestling with braille and the typewriter, after all the tough work with Theo, the words from the bedroom were like daggers in his back.

"Perhaps there's no better solution," muttered Dad, and his voice sounded tired. "I've talked myself hoarse. I've pleaded and begged and promised that we'd be behind Ben one hundred percent."

"The fools."

"Don't say that. We didn't know all the problems . . . "

"But we've promised Ben . . . "

There was a brief silence and Ben heard his mother crying softly.

"Now, now. Come on, tears won't help at all." His father's voice trying to comfort.

"What will help then?"

"Not taking it lying down. Tomorrow or the day after I'm going to the institute to see what the experts have to say."

"Oh, no, not that," said Mother, still half sobbing. "Surely we won't just go by what the rector says?"

"What do you think we should do then?"

"I can go and see the people in the board of education. And I can collect signatures from the parents of the children in Ben's class."

"Signatures?" asked Dad doubtfully.

"That they've no objection to having someone blind in the class."

"Why should they?"

"Because it makes special demands. Because Ben's there the teaching could slow down."

Another silence. Then the flick of a lighter. A last sniff from Mom. Now they were both staring ahead of them, searching for what would be best for their son.

Ben could barely restrain himself from shouting. The whole business left him as cold as an icicle. On top of everything else, now his pride had taken a hard knock. Collecting signatures. He'd rather cut off his right arm.

His mother's voice: "Should we tell him what the rector's said?"

Ben held his breath. The answer would tell him whether or not he could trust his parents from now on.

"I should say so," said Dad quietly.

"Perhaps we should wait for a while. He's got so much to get through just now."

Again a leaden silence.

"If we say nothing, the blow will be all the harder when it comes."

"He'll be very upset." His mother's voice trembled.

"So are we," muttered his father.

The bed creaked. A lighter flicked. A sigh.

Then his mother's voice, as vulnerable as a reed in the wind.

"Tom, could the high school really turn Ben down?"

"I'm afraid so."

"But we have to keep on fighting, even if we have to go to the people at the top."

"Perhaps," said Dad cautiously. "Perhaps."

Again the silence of his parents sitting up in bed smoking, with the uncertain future of their child like an invisible wraith between them.

Ben turned. He'd heard enough. He wanted to be back in his room with his confusion and bewilderment. His parents' discussion seemed to thump through his body and cripple him. He had never felt so deeply aware of their sorrow and concern.

Why couldn't the accident have happened a few years later?

He meant to go back to bed, but in his mood of revolt his blindness was complete. By the door of his room he stumbled over the linen basket and fell.

"Damn!"

The word flew out in rage. He listened. Yes, of course his father and mother had heard him. They leaped out of bed. Bare feet on the floorboards. The door of their room opened.

"Ben!" Mother's voice, frightened and worried. His father took his arm and helped him up.

"Is anything wrong?"

"I was going to the john." A flimsy excuse, but he couldn't think of anything else.

"Come on, then." His mother took over the arm from his father.

"What time is it?"

"After one thirty."

"Weren't you two asleep?"

It seemed a casual enough question, but it was loaded with suspicion. Ben meant to test his parents, for his confidence was still shaken.

"No, we were still awake."

"As late as this?"

"Yes."

Dad's voice was even, but Ben was sure he was looking at Mom.

"We had a lot to talk about."

"About me?"

"Yes, including about you."

"Come," said Mother. "It's so late now."

Ben allowed himself to be led to the lavatory. He didn't need to use it, but he flushed it all the same. He imagined himself being sucked down into the depths with the swishing water. That wasn't such a strange thought. The deepest pits in life are in many ways like a dark, filthy sewer.

Darkness and the stillness of the night. Ben lay on his back. Sleep wouldn't come. He kept thinking of his parents, who hadn't quite told him the truth. Fishing into the murky waters of the sewer, he brought the most somber thoughts to the surface.

Not back to his old school? How unfair it seemed. Hadn't he been among the best pupils in the class? Perhaps, perhaps there was still a chance if they made a fight for it and talked to people in the education department. Would they really have to ask signatures from the parents of his classmates? That nutty Milly, for instance, or that good-for-nothing sneak Norman. He'd rather die. Why, why, hadn't the gardener left his rake by the compost heap on that very day? He brooded grimly over his broken life and the chaos that seemed to fill the whole world.

As he tossed from one side to the other, a kind of horror film unrolled for him. And just as with the black, squirming snakes, he couldn't shut off his mind from it. For the tossing, turning Ben it was a long, dark, despairing night. He felt that his whole existence had been shattered and he didn't have enough strength to pick up the fragments.

*I wish I were dead.* The thought flashed through him. *Then I'd be done with it all. And Mom and Dad too.*

He was still too young to realize that the way to the stars is always through darkness.

Only when a fresh spring day was announced by the cheerful twitter of the birds and by the shunting of an early goods train did Ben finally fall asleep.

A labyrinth of alleys, like an Oriental bazaar. He raced through them, as if death were at his heels. To the left. To the right. Round another corner. And again he came face to face with the fearsome man with the knife. He fled on through the narrow crowded streets, gasping for breath and always aware that the danger was right behind him. But wherever he turned and whatever plan he contrived, there was the man with the knife and the hideous grimace.

"Are you still asleep?" From a great distance he heard his mother's voice.

It was a few moments before Ben bridged the gap between dream and reality. When he had done so, he felt no sense of liberation. The new day fell on him like a wet blanket.

"I've brought your breakfast."

Ben pushed himself up.

"Here's your tea."

Ben took the cup and gulped down some tea.

"What time is it?"

"Quarter past nine."

97

"As late as that already?"

"I let you sleep late after last night." His mother's voice was careful and very motherly.

Did her words bring even more tension in the already tense atmosphere of the room?

"You two were up late as well."

"Yes," said his mother.

"Was anything wrong?"

She hesitated only for an instant. Then she put the tray with his breakfast on the bedside table. Did she realize how important her answer would be?

"Yes, Ben, there was."

"What was it?"

"Dad went to see the rector yesterday."

"And . . . ?"

Ben hated himself for asking when he already knew the answer. Why was it so important to know if Mom would tell the truth or mislead him? Did his faith in her have to be restored?

"And . . . ?" he insisted.

She drew in her breath like someone who had to give a difficult explanation and didn't know how to begin. At that moment the doorbell rang. His mother sprang up like a boxer saved by the bell, thought Ben.

"Now who can that be?" she murmured as she made full speed out of the room.

Ben lay there with his breakfast and a guilty feeling. Why had he made it so unnecessarily difficult for his mother?

The front door opened and a man's voice sounded through the hall.

"A registered parcel. Will you sign, please?"

"Here?"

"Yeah. Lovely day, ma'am, isn't it?"

"It certainly is."

A lovely day. If the mailman only knew, Ben thought, with mounting bitterness. What did it matter whether the sun shone or not? After a long awful night full of disappointment, full of helplessness, full of uncertainty, all he had to look at was the black hole of another day. And yet the deepest pits in life can sometimes be filled up in a few minutes. Just as in snakes and ladders, one throw can lead to safety. Such a chance was about to happen to somber, blinded Ben as his mother came upstairs again.

The minute she came into the room, Ben decided not to ask again what the rector had said. It would only hurt her, and she had enough to bear already, hadn't she?

"There's a package for you."

"A package? For me?"

"Yes, a very small one. Feel it."

Ben put out his hand. The package fitted into his palm. It was tied with string.

"Who sent it?"

"A Mrs. Hill," said Mother, slightly curious.

"Never heard of her."

"There's a letter attached."

"Read it, then. Or is it in braille?"

A cynical joke, to which his mother made no response. She went to the washbasin, picked up the nail scissors, and cut the string. Then the envelope.

Rustle of paper. Silence. She must be reading the letter from Mrs. Hill, whoever she might be.

"Oh, surely not," came Mother's whisper, shocked, dismayed, full of pain.

"What is it?"

"It's a letter from the student in ward three," said his mother quietly, and a shiver crept over Ben's back.

"From him?"

Two shaky words, as unsteady as a baby learning to walk. Mother cleared her throat.

"I'll read it to you," she said and sat down on the edge of the bed.

Dear Ben,
I've begun to write to you three times already, and each time the letter grew so long that the words lost any significance. So, for the third time, very briefly. When you read this letter, I won't be here any longer.

Mother sniffed loudly. The letter lay in her hand.

A deep melancholy swept through Ben. He felt ashamed of last night with its bitterness and rebelliousness. Then his thoughts drifted back to ward three, to the talks with the student who had proved himself such a precious friend and who now was gone.

"Dear God," he whispered brokenly. He bit his lip trying not to cry.

His mother read on in an unsteady voice.

I'm sending you an old watch that my grandfather gave me a few years ago. It strikes the
hour and the half hour, so you'll always be
able to hear the time.

Ben trembled because now there rose very clearly
in his thoughts the image of the student, although
he'd never seen him in the flesh. And he knew that
he was a friend he'd never forget. Yes indeed, a part
of him would live on in Ben, just as the student had
hoped.

Ben, my textbooks have told me that blind
people are sometimes suspicious. That's of
course because they can't see. With all my heart
I want you to go on facing life with absolute
confidence. Nothing is so stifling as suspicion.
Try to love life, even when it lets you down,
and make something of it.

The last words seemed to dissolve in the warm
morning sun shining through the window. Mother
opened the package.

"It's a gold watch, Bennie. A real fat old turnip."
She laid it gently in Ben's hand.

Then Ben could restrain himself no longer. He
didn't want to cry, but an overflow of emotion welled
up in him. The lump in his throat nearly choked
him, but at last he burst out:

"Mother!"

It was as if the grief of weeks now suddenly had
to find an outlet, and he sobbed uncontrollably in

his mother's arms. The student, and the letter, and the whole history behind it filled him with sorrow.

Then suddenly he burst out, between sobs, "I know about the rector. It doesn't matter now."

Mother patted his shoulder, and they sat there together until Ben recovered himself.

"We'll get through all right, Ben."

Ben nodded and sat up straight in bed. He thought about the student, who had known exactly what he intended his letter to do. During a quiet afternoon at the hospital he'd said much the same.

"Ben, in spite of your blindness you belong to the privileged youth of the world. Because your contemporaries in many parts of the earth are far worse off. Think of them sometimes, and keep on loving life in spite of it all, even if it sometimes goes against you."

Ben got out of bed and walked to the window.

"Sorry I let myself go," he said with a last sniff. And then, with more assurance, "It won't happen again."

With a high clear chime the watch struck ten.

# Chapter Nine

LATER, much later, Ben was aware that the student's letter had brought about a big change. The letter and the watch had more or less put an end to his self-pity. Everyone had his own troubles. Wasn't it rather selfish to be so preoccupied by his?

Later, much later, Ben realized that after the letter had been read to him he'd stepped irrevocably over the threshold of his blindness. From then on he faced life with more courage and more awareness, no longer as a handicapped blind boy who had to be treated with respect by everyone, but as an ordinary person who didn't stay apart in his own small corner.

Of course, he often had to defend himself against the outside world, which all too frequently found him pitiful. He had such an experience on that very day, when Mrs. Russell greeted him in compassionate and commiserating tones.

"Oh, Ben, how are you now? It's so terrible for you to be blind. It's simply dreadful."

What do you say to someone like that?

"I'd rather be blind than dumb," Ben had answered, although it wasn't a very polite reply.

In time he learned to respond with a joke.

"I live in blind faith. Everyone can't do that."

Ben could well understand that blindness must be rather frightening to outsiders. He could tell from their voices when people found him pathetic. Then he would say, to put them at their ease,

"Yes, I know it's rotten. But I'm learning to live with it, and did you know I can travel for nothing? All over the place?"

"Honestly? Is that really so?" they'd ask in surprise.

"Yeah—as a blind sightseer."

Although his jokes were pretty feeble, they often produced a bit of relaxation. By means of some humor and self-ridicule Ben could at least demonstrate that he had accepted his blindness.

And, of course, there were other times when gloom got the upper hand. It was lucky that the student's watch always struck the half hour. "Make something of it" was its message, and Ben usually managed to shake off the depression. Wrestling with himself like that, by fits and starts he learned to handle his blindness.

On the other hand, his parents had more and more difficulty in accepting it. Their confusion about their blinded son grew day by day. That too was partly the fault of the outside world.

"How on earth can you even think of an institute for the blind," cried his outraged grandmother. She had come to dinner, and afterward, when Ben and

Maryanne had gone upstairs, she broached the subject of her grandson's future.

"That boy belongs here with you. What he needs now above all is the warmth of this house and your love and care."

In her indignation she dropped her knitting in her lap.

"That's what I think too," said her daughter-in-law. "But . . ."

"There's no 'but' about it," declared Grandma with resolution. She picked up her knitting again as if to signify that the subject was closed.

"It's not so simple." Dad pushed aside a newspaper irritably. "There are problems, Mother, about which you know nothing."

"What kind of problems?"

Father sighed. Of course, she meant well and she only had Ben's good in mind.

"Take braille, for a start," he said wearily. "We've studied books. We've all sorts of material, even an expensive braille machine. But we're not professionals. We can only plod on with it. And that's the question: can it be done by nonprofessionals properly?"

"Ben knows that here he has your love and protection."

"That's beside the point," broke in Father impatiently. "The point is that Ben has to learn braille. And that he's helped as effectively as possible in all his work."

"But you two will do that without question."

Father shook his head. He almost returned to the

attack, but he restrained himself. Hadn't he a few weeks ago been just as shortsighted as his mother? He tried another approach.

"Do you know the size of a fair-sized novel in braille?"

"No."

"It's about thirty thick volumes. Now just imagine that Ben later needs an encyclopedia. In braille all the volumes couldn't fit into his room."

There was no reply from Grandma. Consternation spread over her face like a shadow. For the first time she caught a glimpse of the chasm that had to be bridged by her son and daughter-in-law.

"It's not so simple, you know," said Mother, and her whole expression showed how deeply she felt about the subject. "I thought so, too, at first: Ben will stay at home. We'll pull it off among us. But there are so many problems that Tom and I couldn't take into account. I . . . I don't know now if I coddle and pamper Ben too much much because of his blindness or if I demand too much of him. Things that were so obvious before aren't so any longer. Everything, his whole upbringing, has to be different now."

"Peggy, dear." Grandma was shocked by how emotional her daughter-in-law seemed.

"But it is, it is!" Mother cried almost hysterically. "You treat Ben differently too now. The old relationship's gone. That's why Tom and I have lost our self-confidence. Sometimes I just don't know what to do!" Suddenly Mother burst into tears of despair.

To make matters worse, at that moment Ben came into the room. He heard the sobs.

"What's the matter?" he asked at once. "Why's Mom crying? Have you had a row?"

"Well, eh, you see . . ." Grandma sank into a bog of would-be excuses.

"Yes," said his father quickly. "We had an argument and I said the wrong thing."

Ben heard his father stand up and go over to his mother.

"Sorry," he said softly. "Stop crying now. I really didn't mean to be nasty."

Grandma bit her lip, knowing why Ben's father took the blame for the tears. Wasn't it better for Ben that his mother cried because of a row than because of the blindness of her child?

Grandma looked sorrowfully at her son and daughter-in-law. Then she turned her glance to Ben, who was still standing dead still in the room, and somehow he suddenly looked older.

It is amazing how quickly and carelessly people express an opinion or a judgment. Many acquaintances of the family—not real friends, who knew better—had all sorts of advice about Ben on the tips of their tongues.

"I'd keep him at home," said a well-meaning neighbor across the street. "What good's an institute to a boy like him? Surely he can go on at the high school if he gets the right help?"

"And how do we arrange that?" asked Dad wryly.

"Oh, that must be possible."

"And how do we pay for it?"

"Surely the state takes care of that sort of thing?"

Such a conversation leads nowhere. A cousin of Mother's, who dropped in by chance one day, also had an answer.

"I'd treat him just like any ordinary child. That seems far the healthiest way."

"But being blind's not ordinary," said Mother desperately. "We have to treat him differently from a child who can see. We mustn't make demands that he can't possibly meet."

"Well, as long as you don't let him turn into a moron in some institution or other."

It was then that Dad got angry. He grabbed a cigarette and asked sharply,

"Do you think that every child in an institution is a moron? And do you know how many children are in institutions?"

"Thousands, I guess."

"Hundreds of thousands who are blind, or deaf, or dumb, or spastic, or crippled, or they're orphans. Or the father and mother have been declared unfit. Yes, all children who have something wrong with them. For whom we give generously from time to time. But we keep them safely shut away because we haven't the charity to accept them fully in our society."

"Don't get so excited," whispered Mother.

"And the worst of it is," Father continued, "that I didn't give it a thought myself until recently."

"I know what you mean," muttered the cousin shamefacedly.

"Sorry about the outburst." Dad was shocked by his own emotion. Wasn't he in control of the situation any more? Had he been thrown into confusion by all the contradictory opinions he'd heard from friends and neighbors?

That night, when they were in bed and the light had been put out, Mother took his hand.

"Tom," she said, in a fragile voice. "Will you make an appointment for us tomorrow at the institute for the blind?"

"Yes," Dad whispered.

"Perhaps in the beginning I didn't have the courage to look at everything straight. I needed time to accept the reality. Now I've done it and I'll go by what the experts say is best for Ben."

Father put his arms around her comfortingly.

Ben walked downstairs. In the hall he stopped. For a moment he listened for sounds. It was dead still in the house.

"Granny?"

Bumping noises from the living room. A chair being pushed back. His grandmother came hurriedly into the hall.

"What is it, Ben?"

"When's Mother coming home?"

"Before dinner at the latest. Is anything wrong?"

"I can't go any further with my work."

"Can I do anything?"

"No, thank you." Ben shook his head. If Grandma were to help him with braille, he'd never find the forest for the trees.

"Where's Mom gone?"

"Eh . . . she's gone . . . to a reception with your

father. Someone's left the office after twenty-five years," Grandma improvised. She thought it was better to provide an alibi than to say they'd gone to the institute for the blind. And then, too hastily, she changed the subject. "How about some tea? Or is it too early?"

"In a little while, thanks. I'll take a walk first."

"On your own?" asked Grandma uneasily.

"I do it often."

"Wouldn't you rather that I went along too?"

"No, Granny, that's not necessary."

"Will you be very careful?"

"Yes," said Ben with a sigh, and he picked up his stick.

Grandma would have liked to follow him, but she remembered that Maryanne would be coming home from school any minute. Anxiously she looked after her grandson as he slowly shuffled out of sight.

Perhaps because Grandma had answered so evasively Ben couldn't get their conversation out of his mind. Perhaps too because his parents usually told him where they were going.

As he sat on the bench in the park, Ben had a vague premonition that something was going on and intuitively he knew that it had to do with him.

"Oh, God," whispered Ben in consternation. All his random thoughts flew into place like pieces of a jigsaw puzzle. In a flash he realized what was going on. Of course! There was no possible doubt. Mom and Dad were at the institute for the blind.

The stick fell from his hand. He didn't notice. His

whole small world seemed to have collapsed around him. Now there was only grayness, bewilderment, and a chaos of sensations in which he felt completely lost. Was this the reality he had so long feared? For a moment he lost control. And then the student's watch struck three. Three clear chimes heralded a turning point. An institute for the blind. What if that was the best future for him? His father and mother certainly hadn't gone on the spur of the moment. Ben understood only too well what a difficult step it must have been for them. In his imagination he saw them walking through the gates on their way to the director's office.

"We're right on time," said Father. "It's just three."

Mother didn't respond. She looked at the enormous parking area outside the gate, at the beautifully kept tubs of flowers at the entrance to the institute, at the splendid park lying in light and shadow under the great trees. Ben would never see all that if . . . if he were admitted here. She clasped her husband's arm for support and comfort. They went up to the gate-keeper's lodge.

"My wife and I have an appointment with the director. My name's Lighthart."

"I'll show you where to go."

Father had almost expected a blind gatekeeper, but an elderly woman came out and walked part of the way with them.

"You go between the two buildings. Then you cross the playground. There's a door in the corner and that's the one you want."

Now it was Father who took Mother's arm. He felt tense and nervous. The coming hour would decide Ben's future. But wasn't part of their own life at stake, too?

"Just look at that," whispered Mother, slowing her pace.

Some children were roller-skating in front of the main building. A young teacher watched carefully from the side. From a path to the right came two boys of about sixteen. The first one wore dark glasses. The boy behind held his shoulder with one hand and so let himself be led to the door of one of the side buildings. Perhaps Ben would soon walk here, led in such a fashion by someone who could still see vaguely.

Mother pressed Father's arm closer to her. They walked on. Now they came past a classroom where a teacher sat at work with three children. Mother's eyes flew to the fingers gliding over the sheets of braille: first the fingers of the left hand, then the fingers of the right hand would take over, always anticipating what was to come in the text. She and Ben were miles behind that stage.

They found the right door and went inside. Soon they were standing before the director, a gray-suited man with a pleasant face.

*Thank God for that,* thought Mother. She found him sympathetic right away. He had such calm, understanding eyes.

"Please sit down."

"Thank you."

A restful room with old prints on the walls. Lots of bookshelves. A grandfather clock.

"We've come about our son," said Father, and in bits and pieces they told the whole story.

It was a quarter past four. Father and Mother had asked many questions and the director had answered them all patiently. He had told them about the institute and about education for the blind.

"We have around 120 children here. Some of them are day boarders. They sleep at home and have breakfast there, because for their sakes their parents have found homes in the neighborhood. Most are full-time boarders. They go home on weekends and for vacations."

Father had asked about the various courses. There was a junior school, a high school, a telephone operators training school, a domestic department that taught cooking, handwork, and sewing.

"And, of course, we begin with the kindergarten," the director had said.

"Do they come as young as that?" Mother thought of those blind mites of four or five. What a drama it must be when they were brought from the warmth of home to an institute.

"The younger they are when they begin their blind education, the better it is. Do you know how long it takes to know braille reasonably well—reading, writing, and counting?"

"No, not exactly."

"At least three years. And you, Mrs. Lighthart, are really too old ever to master it now."

To Father's relief, children from the institute attended ordinary schools. Not only textbooks but also the forms that the teaching staff sometimes used for homework or tests were translated into braille in the private printing works.

"But how about subjects like geometry and physics?" In the last weeks Mother had never stopped asking herself how a blind child could ever learn that sort of thing.

"Relief drawings," the director explained. "They do it on braille paper laid over a piece of fine gauze. Of course, they have to be produced in reverse, so that the relief drawings appear in the right way on the pressed-up side of the paper."

"How is it possible," murmured Mother.

"It's very possible indeed. Last week one of our former pupils graduated in math and physics at the Institute of Technology." A certain justifiable pride and satisfaction sounded in the director's voice. Who could estimate what difficulties had been overcome for that degree? It transpired that gifted blind children could choose pretty well any area of study—languages, law, history, psychology.

Little by little, Ben's parents gained some insight into the countless problems that had to be solved in the course of the education of blind children. Much attention was paid to the strengthening of their will-power, self-confidence, powers of endurance, and courage.

"And what do they do in their free time?"

"We have all sorts of hobby clubs. And, of course,

board games like Monopoly are manufactured in braille."

"Sports, too?" A question from Father, who knew it would be important to Ben.

"Yes, sports, too. Judo, riding, swimming, gymnastics, wallball."

"Wallball? What's that?"

"They play it in a hall. Three against three. You have to touch the wall opposite you with the ball while your opponents try to prevent you. There's a bell in the ball, so the players can hear how it rolls. It is fun and excellent training for hearing."

Yet another instance, thought Ben's mother, of how much was involved in the education of a blind child. Hadn't she been naive to imagine that they could do it all on their own?

"We have sports days, too. We organize athletic contests with other blind institutes."

Father and Mother looked at each other. Both now admitted there was only one possibility for Ben's future.

"Have you a place for our son?"

The director nodded.

"We would have liked so much to keep him at home," said Mother softly. "To make a separation like this . . . "

"I know exactly what you mean," said the director. He'd heard this conversation so often before. "That's how it should be—that handicapped children should be able to grow up among other children and not be shut away on their own. But unfortunately that is not yet possible."

And then came the important question that had been foremost in Mother's thoughts and on the tip of Father's tongue:

"Which do you consider better, that a child comes here as a day boarder or full-time?"

"Among other things, that depends on the parents," said the director carefully. "People's attitudes to the blind are mixed. Being blind is not just a problem for the child. It's a tough job too for the father and mother and for brothers and sisters. Many parents lose their natural assurance about upbringing. And there are too few social workers to help them and guide them. In spite of all their goodwill, they sometimes simply go to pieces."

Again Father and Mother looked at each other. Almost relieved. So it wasn't so strange after all that they'd become confused.

"Can he come here, at least temporarily, on a full-time basis?"

At last Father had taken the plunge.

"He can. When did you think of?"

"If it has to be, then as soon as possible," said Mother, and her voice trembled for the first time in the interview.

A quarter of an hour later they were sitting in the car, silent, sunk in their own thoughts, a bit shaken. In many ways it had been a vital, dramatic visit. They had been given a glimpse of a world quite unknown to them. Yet the director had given them the assurance, and the hope, that a blind child, like any other, had a future.

"Our Ben's not the only one," said Father, because he knew how difficult it was for Mother. There were many blind children, although about two-thirds of blind people had lost the power of seeing in old age. Thirty-five million blind people on earth.

"We could try to move nearer to the institute. Then Ben could live at home again," said Father.

"And your work? What about that?"

"I could commute, probably, and if not, then perhaps I can find a job nearer here."

"That's good of you," said Mother gratefully. She was deeply moved. She felt sure now that her marriage didn't hang by a silken thread, but by a stout rope.

They drove off, sitting beside each other in silence. They were both preoccupied by the same problem. How could they, how could they, tell all this to Ben? They had no idea that the problem had been solved in the meantime on a bench in the park.

# Chapter Ten

"CAN IT shut?" asked Dad.

"I think so," answered Mom, throwing a last glance around the room. The suitcase lay packed on the bed. Ben shut it and his father carried it downstairs.

"I'll just comb my hair," said Ben's mother. She touched Ben's cheek in passing as she went out of the room. The last minutes at home. In a little while they'd be leaving.

Ben stood beside his desk in front of the window. He thought of the weeks that lay behind him, and it seemed to him that he'd been on a journey to another part of the world. Or he'd landed in an existence that was completely different. A blind person's part of the world was perhaps a tiny one. All the same the journey had been long and full of tension. A journey through gray darkness, through the depths. But above all a voyage of discovery, because in the past weeks he'd learned so much about himself, people, and life.

When his father and mother had come home from the institute for the blind, Ben had met them at the door. After the difficult moments in the park, he had finally and firmly resolved to accept the inevitable without a struggle. By not making a drama of it, he'd spared himself and his parents a lot of pain. Outwardly at least, it was Theo who protested most against the coming move.

"No, Ben . . . no, you can't mean it."

"We'll see each other on weekends."

"But . . . you can't. We were getting on so well with the work. And what about our paper route?"

Was Theo afraid of fading away into his former isolation?

That morning at breakfast, it was a bit too much for Maryanne, when she had to say good-bye before she went to school.

"So long, Ben, I hope . . . " And she burst into tears.

"Now, then, it's not so awful." Ben tried to comfort her.

"Of course not," Father intervened. "He'll be home every weekend, like lots of boys in training somewhere."

*In training*, thought Ben. How the words expressed what was now awaiting him. And they also indicated what he intended to do later on. He was going to train to help handicapped children. As a psychologist, he was going to help disturbed children to reach a worthwhile human existence. That was his aim. And whoever had a fixed aim in life was never so very unhappy.

The car tooted. They were ready to go. Ben pulled

119

his sweater straight. It was a well-worn gray-purple affair, and he was very fond of it. In spite of Mom's protests, he'd left his suit hanging in the closet. He wanted to make his entrance to the institute as he really was—nothing more, but also nothing less.

Only later did it come to him that it wouldn't make the slightest difference what he had on: probably none of the kids there would be able to see his clothes.

"Come on," called Dad from below.

"I'm coming," answered Mother from her bedroom.

All at once Ben felt his stomach muscles tensing. This was it. He had the feeling that again an episode of his life had come to an end. When he left the hospital it was as if the end of his childhood had come. And now? Now he was going to meet his future; he was standing before a new beginning.

"Well, first I'll take you to your room and then introduce you to the others, or at least as many as are here just now." The director stood up. Ben knew it from the scrape of the chair on the floor.

"Shall we say good-bye here then?" asked Ben, and for a moment it was as though a restless frog had sprung into his throat. The quicker Mom and Dad left, the better. There was no point in prolonging the good-byes.

"So long, Big Ben," said Dad. It was a nickname from long, long ago, and he hadn't heard it for years. Now it seemed to emphasize the bond between them, like the hand on his shoulder and the kiss on his cheek.

"Good-bye, darling. Until Saturday." The last words were meant to show how temporary was the parting. All the same, a frog sprang into Mother's throat, too. She had to get away quickly, she thought, because she wasn't sure if she'd be able to keep on being so calm and brave.

The director held the door open.

"You don't have to show us out. We know the way," said Father.

"Thanks for all your help and good advice." Happily, Mom's voice sounded firmer again. In his thoughts Ben saw them going out and crossing the playground. Dad's arm was surely round Mother's shoulders.

The director had come back into the room and was shuffling some papers on his desk. *He's a nice man*, thought Ben. He liked the calm, businesslike way in which he'd guided the conversation and the farewells. No drama. After all, he wasn't the most pitiful kid in the world, not by far.

"Shall we go?"

"Where's my suitcase?"

"I've got it. Come on, then. Hold my shoulder."

They walked through the hall to the door and went outside. Ben heard high, excited children's voices in the distance. Was the kindergarten coming out? The director stopped.

"Sorry, I've forgotten something. Wait here for a minute, will you? I'll be back in a minute."

Ben stood there by himself in the playground. He listened to the jubilant voices of the children. They sounded just like the children in the park at home.

"My father's bought a yacht!"

"And my father's got a trailer. That's far better—you can go everywhere with it."

"With a yacht, too!"

"Yes, but it can capsize in a storm."

"But with a trailer you can have a crash on the highway."

It was as if Billy and Johnnie the king were there in the distance. Grinning to himself, Ben thought gladly that there wasn't so much difference between blind and sighted children. Probably they had as much joy and as much sorrow. As much boasting, as much fantasy, as much fear.

"Hello, are you new here?" The clear voice of a girl by his side.

He hadn't heard her come up to him.

"Yes, I've just come. I'm Ben Lighthart."

"I'm Tinka." It sounded like the half-hour stroke of the student's watch. "Molly's with me. She's in the infants' class. I'm at the high school myself."

"Did you cry when they left you?" asked Molly.

"No," said Ben.

"I did when I came. I cried buckets."

Ben didn't know what to say to this small creature of five.

Wasn't he privileged, that he'd only just come here?

"How did you know I was here?" he asked curiously. "Can you see?"

"Just a little bit still," answered Tinka, and Ben thought her voice was the sweetest he'd heard in ages. "First I was at a school for poor-sighted children, but my eyes got worse and worse. So I've been here for six months. The doctor says I may be able to get a good eye later on."

"Do you like it here?"

"Oh, yes. I had to get used to it at first, of course. It's different from home. But you learn so much here, you know, that's useful later on."

To Ben's disappointment, for he'd have been glad to talk longer with Tinka, the director came to fetch him.

"Sorry, that took longer than I expected. There was a call from a parent." He picked up the suitcase, and Ben gripped his shoulder again.

" 'Bye, Ben," said Tinka. "We'll bump into each other again."

"Sure thing," said Ben. He hoped so.

The director led him across the playground. They came to a house next to the main building where he'd have his own room. *The worst is over,* thought Ben. He saw the way to the future ahead of him. He took the first steps along it as he walked into his second home.

# The Author

JAAP ter Haar has an international reputation for his children's books, which have been translated into eight European languages. During the Second World War, he joined the Dutch resistance movement and later became a war correspondent. Some of these experiences were incorporated into his book *Boris*, which won the prize for the best children's book of the year in Holland. Jaap ter Haar has also written many radio and television plays and documentaries, as well as fiction. He lives in Holland and is the father of four children.